CENTAURI MIDNIGHT

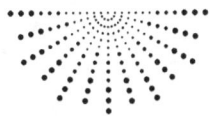

CYNTHIA WOOLF

CHAPTER ONE

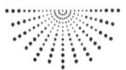

"*A*udra, please. You're my queen but you're also my friend. You must grant me this last request. Let me go after him." Tensign Kiti Dolana paced the beautiful sitting room. Bile rising in her throat threatened to strangle her. Finally, she collapsed into the chair it's soft cushions swallowing her as she sat across the small, highly polished and gleaming, coffee table from the Queen of Centauri, her friend.

The Queen's beautifully distended tummy disallowed much frivolous movement, so she reclined on the couch. She sat up to pour the tea but had trouble reaching the tea pot in the middle of the coffee table. "Kiti would you pour our tea, I'm a bit like a beached whale right now." Audra was anything but a beached whale. Kiti knew the colloquial term from her study of Earth.

Her queen was radiant. Her long, chestnut hair

falling in waves to her waist was gathered on one side of her head. Her clear gray eyes shone bright in her pale face. She wore a beautiful royal purple empire waisted dress that highlighted her pale features. She was beautiful. Kiti remembered a time, on their way back to Centauri from Earth, when she'd not thought so, because she was jealous.

That was before Audra's marriage to Darius and when she'd still be betrothed to Anton. Kiti had been in love with Anton, at least she thought she was, and was jealous of Audra. Some of the things she said were unkind, but Audra had seen them for what they were, jealousy and forgiven her the words. They were now the best of friends.

Kiti poured the tea and continued to beseech her queen. "Audra, you have to let me go after him. He killed my brother Joridan, his actions led to Anton being captured and tortured. I need to see they get justice, they deserve it."

"And you are sure it is only justice you seek?" Audra softly asked.

"Damn it, Audra." Kiti was up and pacing the room again. Her long black hair was tied in a high pony tail and swung back and forth with each step she took. The thick, plush carpet kept her boots from clicking on the floor. "I'm begging you to let me go with Garrick Marcus. It's not just revenge I need. I need closure. I'm the one who should deliver Tybold to the authorities. Garrick Marcus is the best captain in the fleet and I know Darius is sending him after Tybold. Joridan needs us both to avenge his death. To bring his murderer back to Centauri for justice to be served."

"Kiti, are you combat trained? We don't know what to expect from the Proconians. By this time, Tybold could have convinced them we are conquerors and he's their only salvation. We don't know. It could be a suicide mission. I don't want to lose my best friend." She went on. "I know you're grieving. Joridan's loss and Lara's return has been very hard on you."

"Stop." Kiti jumped up and started to pace again. "I know what my life has been like. I mourn the loss of Joridan life and Anton's capture and torture by Slavarien. Joridan was my little brother. Even though he was a head taller than me he will always be my little brother. I still smell Joridan's scent in his room. Sometimes it's so fresh it's like he just passed by." Her eyes filled with tears, "I miss the closeness that Anton and I once shared but I do not bemoan him finding Lara. I'm very happy he found his lifemate. It was something he never thought to be able to do. After the torture that both Anton and Lara suffered at the hands of the Slavariens, it's amazing that they found each other. I wish I had a lifemate out there somewhere.

"Audra, I'm a historian and anthropologist, but first I'm Dragonera. Of course, I am combat trained. All Dragonera are. We are the Royal Guard. We are the best."

"Yes. You're right, but I worry anyway. Must be my maternal instinct." Audra patted her belly.

"You know that the people of Procon are centuries behind us technologically. I'm the only person who can go on this mission that knows anything about their culture."

"I don't know," Audra hesitated.

"Admit it. Garrick needs me."

"We don't interfere in the development of other planets' civilizations. You know that."

"Tybold has already interfered. I say we'll be evening the odds for the tribes involved. And it's not as though Procon doesn't know we exist. They already trade with other planets. Just because they're not our technological equals doesn't mean they aren't advanced."

Kiti saw Audra hesitate before she answered. "I must confer with Darius before I can give you my answer."

At that moment Darius came in accompanied by Garrick, Anton and Lara. The three men were in their Dragonera uniforms as was Kiti. The only differences being the color blocking. Darius and Garrick wore amethyst uniforms with cream colored sleeves, denoting their status as starship Captains. Darius' uniform also had a cream colored stripe from the left shoulder to the waist, denoting that he was Captain of the Royal Guard. As a general in the Royal Army, Anton's uniform was solid amethyst. Lara, Audra's twin sister, still had the tanned skin from someone who's spent too much time in the sun. She wore the House of Danexx royal colors like everyone else did. Hers were an amethyst jumpsuit and long cream colored duster. Kiti's uniform was solid cream. Her rank as Tensign was denoted by a patch on her left arm.

"What do you need to discuss with me?" Darius asked as he took his wife's arm and helped her to rise from the couch. She gave him a quick kiss. Darius rubbed her stomach then bent and said, "Hello, my children. Are you being nice to your mommy today?"

Kiti swore he expected an answer.

"If you don't quit that people are going to think you're crazy," said Audra.

Darius laughed and kissed her belly.

"I am. Crazy in love with my wife."

Lara made gagging sounds. 'Will you two remember that you have an audience?"

"All right. But you and Anton are just as bad as we are." Darius said to his soon to be twice over sister-in-law."

"Never," retorted Lara. "No one is as over the moons as you two.

"I don't know, I'm pretty much over the moons about you," said Anton waggling his eyebrows at her.

The banter was not aimed at Kiti. She didn't think the two couples even remembered they were not alone. Kiti glanced at Garrick, who rolled his eyes at her.

"Audra, the mission." She reminded her queen tapping her wrist to hurry her.

"Oh yes. Darius, Kiti has requested to be assigned to go with Garrick to Procon, to apprehend Lord Tybold. I told her I would discuss it with you."

"I don't know if she will be needed," Darius responded.

Garrick spoke for the first time since entering the room. "I think an anthropologist would be very useful on this particular mission. Tensign Dolana would be a definite asset to me in bringing in Tybold."

"Thank you, Garrick. " Kiti was warmed by his words and agreed with him one hundred percent. To her way of thinking, this mission would only succeed with her help. No one could understand the Proconians better than she could.

"Very well," said Darius. "You will receive your orders tomorrow. In the mean time, can we eat dinner? I'm a starving man."

CHAPTER TWO

iti was more than ready to leave when she'd received the order to report. She was a historian and anthropologist but she was also, a Tensign in the Army, which meant she had to await orders like anyone else. Her personal relationships with Anton and Audra did not change her position in the service.

She left immediately for the space dock station. By air car it would take thirty minutes to reach the spaceport, then another fifteen to check in before she got to the ship. Her orders gave her two hours to report. There was no time to stop and smell the roses, to use an old Earth saying. Just one of many she'd been required to learn when they went to retrieve Audra just a few months ago.

She meant to be there in plenty of time to be settled in her quarters and on the bridge for the undocking.

She'd heard Garrick always took out the ship himself and it could be quite exciting.

Garrick saw Kitari as soon as she came on the bridge. He was acutely aware of her no matter where they were. He'd kept his feelings to himself since she and Anton were lovers for years. But he always felt her, smelled her special scent in the room even if she wasn't in there anymore. He'd kissed her once at a party celebrating the passing moons. He still tasted her sweetness on his lips. Felt her soft curves against the hard planes of his body. He'd been tempted, so very tempted, to take her and make love to her, but she'd still been reeling from the losses of both Joridan's life and Anton's companionship. It would've been unconscionable for him to take advantage of her in that state of mind.

But Anton had found his lifemate in Lara. Now they were the King and Queen of Delaz and busy rebuilding the country after they'd ended the Slavarien family's reign of terror.

Kiti was meant for him. Garrick's patience was nearly at an end! When the opportunity to go after the traitor Lord Tybold presented itself, Garrick volunteered to lead the mission. He'd wanted to get away from Kiti before he embarrassed himself with declarations of love that she wasn't ready for. His heart leapt when he heard Darius give her permission to join the task force that Garrick was leading. She was going to be on the mission with him. He would be working closely with her for the two week trip to Procon. Together they would learn about Procon and if he had his way they would learn about each other as well.

Kiti was grieving. Her brother and only living family had died in the ambush organized by Lord Tybold. That one bloody battle had taken both of the men in her life, Anton and Joridan, from her. The losses were in different ways it was true, Joridan's life and Anton's freedom and eventually his love.

Garrick wouldn't take advantage of her grief and he'd see to it that no one else did either. Though he would make sure she knew he was interested and available. He intended to court her. It was old fashioned, but something she might appreciate.

"Captain Marcus." Kiti approached and gave a smart salute. "Tensign Dolana reporting for duty."

"Welcome aboard the **Dremel**, Tensign. We are about to leave space dock. Would you like to stay on the bridge?"

"Aye, Captain. I would like that very much." Garrick was pleased by her enthusiasm. He liked having her close. She watched the nav screen and he watched her. He'd done this so many times he could do it with his eyes closed now.

Garrick took command of the navigation console and manually maneuvered the great ship from the dock. He accelerated at the start, bringing her about, hard starboard and at the last minute releasing the moorings.

He heard Kiti's sharp intake of breath and smiled. It was always that way with first timers

"Don't worry, Tensign," he assured her. "I've done this a few times before."

"Why would I worry?"

Her bravado pleased him.

"Mr. Samyod, you have the helm. Take us to full impulse power till we are out of our system, then increase to warp four."

"Aye, Captain," replied Mr. Samyod, Garrick's navigation officer.

"Tensign Dolana accompany me, please."

"Aye Captain."

Kiti followed him into the lift. His heart was beating so hard he was sure she could hear it.

After the lift doors locked, Garrick said, "Kiti, how are you? I see you got your orders and made it in plenty of time so see us leave space dock. My guess is you were already packed when your orders came."

She relaxes against the cool wall of the lift. Comfortable now with her friend not her captain.

"Of course, I was packed. I know Darius. He was hoping I'd miss the takeoff and have to stay out of harms' way."

"He has your best interest at heart."

Kiti laughed. "Ha! He has Audra's best interest at heart. Specifically, she would be heartbroken if anything happened to me. But Audra needs to understand that first, I am Dragonera, with all the rights and responsibilities that entails."

"I'm sure Darius explained that to her, after we were out of ear shot."

"You're right of course." She let out a sigh. "I seem to be set off by the least little thing lately. I'm just surviving until I have avenged Joridan's murder. Surviving is all I can do right now."

"That's not true. Joridan would not want you to live only for revenge. You are too loving and full of life...."

"I don't know, Garrick." She looked up into the concerned face of her friend. When had he grown so handsome. His dark blond hair was full on top and short in the back, perfect for her to run her fingers through. She pictured herself tousling it after wild love making. Good grief, where was that coming from. This was Garrick, her friend. Her gorgeous, friend with the bulging biceps and chocolate brown eyes. She got her thoughts back to his comment. "The fun loving part of me, died with Joridan. I don't think I can ever get that part of me back again. I'm bitter and I know it. I'm trying to get past it, I have good days and bad just like I'm sure you do."

"We've been friends for many years. I know you. It'll take time, but you will return to the Kiti we all know and love, eventually."

She glanced up, question in her beautiful green eyes. Was it because he'd said he loved her? Or hope because he'd said she'd return to being herself?

He glossed over it quickly, as the lift door slid silently open. "Why don't you have dinner with me tonight? To catch up. There hasn't been a lot of time to just talk in the last few months."

"I'd like that."

"Good, I'll come to your quarters at eight o'clock," said Garrick.

"Fine. See you then."

Garrick watched her leave for the library, where she would be doing her in depth research on the peoples of Procon.

He set out for the botanical gardens and wondered if they'd notice a dozen roses missing? Kiti would appreciate their fragrance and could use the cheering up.

At eight o'clock on the nose, he rang the buzzer to Kiti's quarters.

"Come in." He heard as the door slid open. "I've ordered some appetizers and," she said with great fanfare, "I have a bottle of the family's special noskberry wine from Audra."

"I'm jealous. She's never gifted me with one of her precious bottles." Then he smiled wide. "I'm honored you'd share it with me."

She'd laid out the appetizers on the small low table in front of the sofa and had opened the wine to let it breathe.

"Would you pour?" she asked.

Garrick filled the glasses half way and handed her one. He raised his glass. "Here is to good friends and a successful mission."

"To good friends and justice for our departed loved

ones." She said before she drained her glass. "So, what are our plans?"

Garrick sat back on the cool, leather couch, his body angled toward her. "Once we get to Procon, I'll send a landing party point team, to gather intel on Lord Tybold. We need to know what he's been up to these last few months since he fled Anton's forces."

She took a sip of the sweet, fragrant wine. The berry flavor, rested on her tongue and invaded her senses. "We must determine which tribe Tybold has aligned himself with and then determine who their enemies and allies are. I've been studying the research that we currently have available. It appears that there are three main tribes on Procon. The Nerutas who rule in the north, the Zolthor in the west and the Otula in the east. The south is mostly deserted and is no man's land, inhabited by small bands of outlaws."

"Tell me what you know about each of them," Garrick said. "We need to decide which one Tybold is most likely to have approached. Then we won't have to recon each tribe."

"I disagree. We need to learn as much as possible about each of them, in order to know their strengths and weaknesses. I can give you a better idea about each tribe once I've had time to do more research. Right now, my preliminary information indicates that Nerutas are the most likely to accommodate Tybold. They are the most aggressive of the three and the most war like. They would definitely want the weapons Tybold has to offer."

"So the Zolthor and the Otula are allies?"

"You'd think so, common enemy and all, but that doesn't seem to be the case. Whereas they both will war on Nerutas, they will also go to war with each other if provoked. Then there are the nomadic desert dwellers, who are at war with no one and act as negotiators when needed. It's really a very interesting dynamic," explained Kiti.

"What type of government does each have? Are they monarchies?"

"No. The leadership is earned through combat. I believe that Zolthor has the best potential for what we need. They are the most stable of all three of the main tribes. The current leaders, called the Valmud, have been winning the challenges for the last six generations. Not only are they smart but also they've brought their people's technology forward twice as fast at the other two. They're the strongest of the three, but also the least likely to accommodate Tybold." Kiti warmed to her subject. She'd done a lot of research and it was all she could do not to be jumping up and down with the information. *It was so nice to be able to talk to someone again. Garrick had always been a good listener, she just never realized he was such a handsome listener. It was almost enough to make her tongue tied. What she wouldn't give to be using her tongue on a certain part of his anatomy. Good grief, Kiti, what has gotten in to you?*

"Why do you say that?"

She came out of her reverie and back to the conversation. If Garrick, noticed her lapse he didn't mention it. "Everything I've read indicates they are an honorable people. Honor above all. That wouldn't fit with Tybold, who as we know has no honor. Tybold will have tried to gain their trust though. He can appear to have honor when it suits him. They control the largest of the known kalcion deposits."

"I knew it was a good idea to bring you with us," Garrick praised. "Kiti, you've provided us with more information than we could have gathered through a month of observation alone."

"Thank you," Kiti said, with not a little pride. "But my only reason for coming on this mission is to apprehend Tybold. He's got to pay for what he did."

"I agree. What do we have for dinner? Can we talk about things other than the mission?"

"Sure. Though you may have to remind me. When it comes to Joridan and making Tybold pay, I tend to be single minded." Kiti led the way to the small, square dining table. She'd put the roses in a large glass container in the center of the table and stopped to sniff their sweet fragrance again. She couldn't seem to get enough of it. "I thought we'd try one of Audra's favorite meals. Her mother Maggie's recipes are in the computer and the food synthesizer can whip it up for us. It's called "chicken fried steak with mashed potatoes and gravy."

They looked at each other and shrugged. Both of

them had tried some of the recipes that Maggie had brought back from Earth. This was a new one.

After they'd eaten their fill of the delicious gravy covered deep fried meat and mashed potatoes, Garrick said, "That's not bad. I think Maggie could teach the palace chefs a thing or two."

They laughed, shared some stories about their friends and finished the bottle of noskberry wine. By the time Garrick got up to leave, Kiti felt a little tipsy and a whole lot horny. It'd been a very long time since she'd had sex.

So when Garrick leaned down to give her a kiss on the cheek, she turned her head and caught him smack on the lips. He moved to pull away, seemingly surprised by her boldness, but she would have none of it. She grabbed the back of his head and brought his lips back to hers. Garrick gave up his resistance and kissed her deeply, before he broke the kiss and rested his forehead against hers.

CHAPTER THREE

*K*iti. We can't. I don't want to be rebound sex for you."She pulled away from him, stung by the truth of his words. "I'm sorry Garrick. I…I don't know what got into me."

He caressed her cheek. "Don't mistake my reluctance as rejection. I very much want to make love to you. But when I do," he took his knuckle and lifted her chin until she looked him direct in the eyes, "it will be because you want to make new memories, not forget old hurts." With that he kissed her hard and left His scent remained and her body ached.

Kiti reeled. Garrick wanted her for more than just a tumble between the sheets. He knew about Anton and didn't seem to mind. Did he really care for her? Could he love her? That kind of thing just didn't happen. At least not to her.

Everyone assumed that she'd been devastated when

Anton and Lara announced their marriage. In fact, she'd been relieved. What did that say about her? Had she been with Anton only because he was convenient, because he was familiar? She supposed that many successful marriages were based on those traits. But she wanted more.

She wanted it all.

The kiss that Garrick gave her hinted at the "more". Was it possible the love of her life had been this close all the time and she'd been too blind to see him? Or was he only a rebound? Was she reading more into his words than he meant? Was all this just the wine talking? She wished she knew.

Damn!! What the hell had he been waiting for?

CHAPTER FOUR

*N*ow Kiti was torn. Garrick wanted to be more than just a friend. She could easily get him to have sex with her, but what was it he said? "Because you want to make new memories not forget old hurts."

She wasn't ready for that kind of commitment. Was she? Could she forget the past? The known is always easier to accept than the unknown.

But he was right. Until she was able to put the past behind her, there could be no future. Not with Garrick, not with anyone. She did want a future. She wanted someone who loved her as much as she loved him. Anton had found his true love. And though she was truly happy for him, she was also jealous and angry. She'd spent her whole life with Anton, someone who knew she wasn't the person he would marry. She'd known it too. She lied to herself and the rest of the world when she said she was fine. She wasn't fine, she was hurt and mad as hell at the whole situation. She wanted more than a one night stand of fulfilling but mindless sex.

No. She wanted more, Garrick was right about that, but what did she want?

That was easy. She wanted a lifetime of it. She wanted everything.

Husband, children, happy and secure home. Yes, she wanted it all.

It had taken all of Garrick's will power not to make love to Kiti right there on the floor of her quarters. If he hadn't walked away…. It had been too close. His goal was not one night or even one month with her. He wanted a lifetime, twenty lifetimes. Forever. He wanted eternity.

His plan was just getting started. It would take nearly two weeks to reach Procon. He could do a lot of wooing in two weeks.

*Z*ia collapsed against Tybold's chest. His now flaccid cock still within her.

"You always take everything I've got to give," he rasped in her ear. "And then milk me for more."

"I'm greedy," she replied as she tightened, released and tightened her inner muscles again, literally milking him to erection again. She moved against him rubbing her body up and down his. Then she lifted her upper body till she was riding him, up and down, with each movement more friction, more momentum, until he was hard inside her, thrusting upward to each of her downward strokes.

"Who do you love?" she demanded on her upward stroke, holding herself up till he answered.

"You," he panted. She slammed her body down, squeezing him tight within her vagina.

"Who will be your queen?" she demanded again with the next stroke.

"You, only you."

She knew he was hurting now. His need for release was nearly overwhelming and she could only push him so far.

"What are you going to do for me?" Each upward stroke she squeezed, her muscles straining to be just a little tighter each time.

"Anything, anything. Just stop this torture."

She took pity on him and pumped her body up and down until she felt him stiffen beneath her and with one last upward thrust, his cum pulsed into her.

*G*arrick put his plan into action. Every day he made sure to join Kiti in the library. He'd have their lunch delivered by a member of the kitchen staff. Although each crew member had a food synthesizer in their quarters, Garrick encouraged them to take their meals together in the cafeteria. He didn't want any of them to become too isolated. Taking meals together encouraged communication and cooperation. It was one of the reasons his crew was the best in the fleet.

The ship's kitchen had the best chefs available, second only to those in the royal palace. He chose something special every day, usually one of Maggie's recipes from her time on Earth.

Maggie had already adapted them to use Centauri meat and produce, but the synthesizers could make them almost exactly as the original recipe was written.

He spoke with Dr. Passdar, the ships botanist, about being able to get a dozen flowers every day. She agreed, but said they could not be roses. She was still not happy about the ones he'd stolen.

Therefore, one day he'd have daisies, the next carnations, each day different from the previous one. The best day was the orchids. He thought Kiti would fall into his arms and declare her love for him. Instead, she'd hugged him and kissed him hard on the mouth, giving him a tantalizing taste of things to come. She turned away so fast his arms were holding only air by the time he moved to embrace her, yet he couldn't have been more pleased.

His slow, by Centauri standards, courting of her seemed to be working. Each time they had dinner, Kiti was more sexily dressed than the time before. Each day they had lunch and if he hadn't been with her for dinner the night before, there was an excitement she couldn't hide. Her smile was brighter, her skin flushed and her eyes sparkled like jewels. Those beautiful exotic, unique green eyes. He'd never met anyone else with eyes the color of Kiti's. Joridan had green eyes but they were much lighter. No one ever came close to the dark, clear green of Kiti's eyes.

Garrick was having a very difficult time keeping his hands, lips and other parts of his anatomy off her delectable body. Patience, he told himself. Patience.

He would keep things casual; let her anticipation build, though it felt like he was punishing himself. All he really wanted to do was take her in his arms and kiss her senseless. He could wait. The reward was too great.

*K*iti took extra time getting ready. She piled her long black hair high on her head revealing her graceful neck, ripe for kissing. The knee length red vest she wore lent a pale blush to her creamy white skin. A low cut black jumpsuit emphasized her lush curves and would send Garrick over the edge.

She brought out another bottle of the noskberry wine that Audra had given her. If ever there was a special occasion this was it.

Tonight, Garrick would succumb to her charms or her name was not Kitari Dolana.

Kiti greeted Garrick and answered his usual questions about her day. "I've been studying all the mentions of the kalcion metal mined on Procon. We use it for decoration, but in large quantities it could be used as starship hulls, engine components and as shields on those same ships. It's stronger and lighter than anything we currently use.

"The only reason I can see that we don't use it more is lack of raw material. We don't have any trade agreements with Procon, which is a mistake and one that Tybold is bound to exploit."

Garrick agreed. "If Tybold gets a monopoly on the kalcion, think of what he could do, what he could extort from Centauri."

"He's got to be stopped and brought to trial for his crimes," said Kiti. "He can't be allowed to profit from Joridan's murder."

"We will apprehend him, Kiti. I promise."

When had he moved so close? She smelled his clean aftershave and some other scent that was, she suspected, unique to him. His uniform was the colors of the House of Danexx, amethyst and cream. The dark purple body of the uniform did nothing to hide the hard, muscled body underneath. And those cream colored sleeves only emphasized his incredible biceps. It was enough to send Kiti into a swoon, if she'd been a weak-willed girl.

Tonight Kiti had a plan. She was not oblivious to Garrick's wooing ways. In fact, she was very flattered he'd taken the time and done the research to find out about how it was done on Earth. She was sure he didn't understand how very much it meant to her. For someone go to such lengths was amazing. She felt special for the first time in a very long time.

"I have something special." She pointed to the noskberry wine resting on the table. "I got more than one bottle from Audra." She grinned at him.

"Ah, so not only have I not gotten one bottle now I will have to complain that I didn't get two."

Kiti winced. "Oh, poor baby. Would it help if I told you I begged for them?"

Garrick laughed. "Actually, I am again, very honored you'd share it with me. I'm not sure I would have, had they been mine."

She brightened and smiled. "You're teasing. You would've shared them with me. You're never serious."

"You're wrong about that," he said, his voice dark with promise. "I'm very serious when I say that I want you."

She could feel her flush creep up her cheeks. Her heart fluttered at his words. Flattered beyond reason, she poured him a good sized portion. She couldn't get him drunk, not on one bottle of wine, but she might be able to get under his defenses. She was determined that one way or another she would make love with him tonight. Determined to go forward and leave the past behind, she was ready to make new memories, with Garrick.

"I've arranged with Chef to have Audra's favorite 'pot roast' tonight. She liked it so much that she'd ask Maggie to make it to celebrate her birthday. Then, there was the carrot cake that Maggie made that was to die for, according to Audra. We don't have carrots but according to Maggie sunda roots are an acceptable substitute."

"You've gone to a great deal of trouble for tonight's dinner and before you think me totally blind, I must tell you how absolutely ravishing you look tonight."

Kiti was flooded with warmth. "Thank you. You don't look so bad yourself, Captain Marcus."

Garrick took the wine bottle from her and set it on the table, probably wondering what she was up to.

"Garrick, tomorrow we reach Procon."

"Yes, we do. I was going to make sure you were aware."

"I am and I want to be in the initial landing party."

"No."

"Garrick, please listen to me before…"

"No. It is much too dangerous."

Kiti set her wineglass on the table in front of her. She went to Garrick, wrapped her arms around his waist and waited for him to reciprocate. When he did and his arms were tight around her, she leaned back until she was looking directly up into his eyes of warm brandy. She let go of his waist, trusting he would not let her fall, worked her hands slowly up his chest, caressing every inch as she went, then wrapped them around his neck

"Please." She said pulling his head down to her.

"No."

"Please," her lips whispered against his.

Garrick groaned. "Kiti you don't know what you're doing to me."

Her voice was as deep and sultry as she could make it. "Yes, I do." She kissed him softly. "I want to remember, Garrick. I want to think of the future not the past." She kissed him again. Her tongue teased the seam of his lips.

He groaned again before opening his mouth to her tender assault. She kissed him hard, deep, her tongue dueling with his.

He gathered her in his arms and made his way to the bed. Though not really more than a plank sticking out of the wall with a mattress and comforter on it, it would do. She slipped down his body eliciting moans as she slid over his erection.

The vest was the first to go, sliding off her shoulders and arms to the floor. Next was the jumpsuit she knew was driving him crazy, fitting her in all the right places as it did. He unfastened it, let it slide to the floor, revealing her high, creamy breasts to his vision.

"Thank Krios," he said on a sigh. "I thought I'd

never get to your luscious breasts. He took one erect nipple in his mouth, suckled and tongued it making her legs weak. Her legs collapsed under her just as his arms came around her for support.

Her wits returned enough for her to realize he was still dressed and she frantically pulled and pushed at his clothes until his magnificent body was naked as hers was. Seeing every lean muscle, his taunt stomach and long muscular legs was enough to send her over the edge. But his cock, standing at attention in its full glory, made her wet. She felt that if she didn't get that glorious piece of his anatomy inside her now she would explode.

Kiti pushed Garrick on to his back on the bed and came down over him. "I need you. In me. Now." She straddled him and was about to get his cock where she wanted, when he grabbed her arms and said, "Slow down, Kiti. We have all night, love. All night. I promise."

His words did not soothe her inner animal. She fell against his chest and moved restlessly, wrapped her legs around him and rubbed against him mimicking the rhythm she would soon wring from his body. "We can be slow later. Now. Garrick. I need you now."

She knew he was undone, his own inner animal, the one he'd leashed so successfully before was now free. His resistance was nonexistent as he rolled her under him and found her wet warmth. He thrust into her. One single stroke and he was buried to the hilt. Kiti moved and arched against him, wringing more from him and herself than she ever been able to feel before.

Garrick kissed her, savored her and Kiti responded in kind. Moving with him, feeling him deep inside her, she welcomed him.

Kiti pulled Garrick's head up and captured his lips with hers. Then she threaded her fingers through his hair and brought him close, touching, skin to skin, heart to heart. He pressed kisses along her neck, making her shiver with delight. Each shiver made her tighten around him, causing a groan to emanate from him that was swallowed by her kiss.

He thrust again and again, slamming against her. She heard as well as felt their bodies slap together. Each plunge brought her closer to the pinnacle. Finally, Garrick reached between their bodies and tickled her swollen, sensitive clitoris. She was so primed; he'd barely touched her when she shattered in his arms.

It was all Garrick needed to follow her into ecstasy.

Lying entwined in each other's arms, her breathing finally returned to normal, Kiti said to him, "I never knew making love could be like that."

Garrick kissed her forehead and hugged her closer. "I didn't either. It's never been like that for me. I've never been out of control before. Never totally lost myself in someone else."

"Stay with me tonight." she said.

"Of course." He hugged her tight to side. "You don't think we're done yet do you?"

"Well, I thought you might," she hesitated, "want to leave now that…"

"Kiti. I don't want to leave."

"I'm glad. How about some dinner?"

"I think I'd rather skip to dessert," he said as he pulled her beneath him.

"Oh my!"

CHAPTER FIVE

*T*he ***Dremel*** took up orbit around Procon. The landing party consisted of Garrick, Kiti and four additional Dragonera. Kiti, was a thoroughly trained member of the Dragonera and also a historian and anthropologist. For that reason, Garrick let her come along, though she knew from their verbal sparring last night that he really wanted to demand she stay safely on the ship.

Being an anthropologist, she'd studied these people just as she had the people of Earth. She once had requested assignment to the planet Procon, in order to study the tribes there. Her grandmother had been adamantly against it. Kiti had argued and was set to leave when her grandmother had become ill and refused to let the med-techs work on her any more. She said she was long past due and was ready to join Grandpa. Then there was Joridan, who was still in school. Kiti couldn't go off and leave him alone, so she'd never gone, never tried to fulfill her dream. Until now.

They transported down just outside the Zothorian capital, if the intel was correct. The computer indicated this to be the largest concentration of dwellings in the Zolthor controlled area.

Almost immediately they were surrounded.

"Don't move" one of the warriors said.

Kiti and Garrick raised their hands and the rest of the team followed suit.

The tallest of the warriors stepped forward. "Tybold said others would follow. The man was a good half a foot taller than Garrick, who at 6'6" already made Kiti feel petite at her 5'10" height. He had white blond hair and sky blue eyes that made a girl want to weep with envy. Kiti would have had to have been dead not to notice and be attracted to the man. She definitely was not dead, though she did her best to mask her reaction after seeing the urge to kill on Garrick's face.

"You speak Centaurian very well," said Garrick through gritted teeth.

The warrior reached up to the translator on the sash that crossed his chest. "The only useful gift from Tybold."

Kiti bit her lip in order not to interrupt and could no longer stand it. "Where is Tybold? Do you have him in custody?"

"Why would we have your emissary in custody?"

"He is not our emissary. He is nothing but a murderer and a traitor." Kiti barely contained her rage.

Blue eyes smiled. "A warrior woman who speaks the truth." He nodded to his men and they lowered their weapons. "I am Peligro, Talmud of the Zolthor. Welcome."

Garrick stepped to Kiti's side. "I am Garrick Marcus, Captain of the **Dremel** and this," he moved closer to Kiti, wanting to show the warrior that she was not available for claiming, "is Kitari Dolana, historian and anthropologist."

"She is your wife also? Or perhaps your mistress?"

"No," said Kiti. "I am not his wife."

Garrick glared at her.

"Or his mistress."

Peligro's grin widened. "You are unclaimed."

"If you mean unmarried, then yes. If you mean, as I think you do, that I am untaken, then no. I am no man's for the taking."

Peligro laughed. "You are mistaken, sharmia, you are already taken." He nodded knowingly at Garrick, who'd quit frowning.

Kiti now frowned at the two men. "Don't call me your 'little one'. I haven't been sharmia for many years…I--"

Garrick cut her off. "If you are willing we would like to begin negotiations for trade but first and foremost we must apprehend Tybold and return him to Centauri for trial."

"Trade discussion will have to be brought before the council of elders. Tybold is another matter. I will personally help you to arrest him and his companion, Zia."

It was Kiti's turn to growl this time. "*Zia* is with him?"

"Yes," replied Peligro. "If she is a beautiful woman with golden hair and a black soul."

"She is. And a wanted criminal as well."

"I would invite you aboard our ship if you are willing," said Garrick. "I understand you may be hesitant, especially after dealing with Lord Tybold. Our prime directive is not to interfere with cultures less advanced than our own."

Peligro began to laugh…and laugh…and laugh.

The more he laughed the angrier Kiti got. She had one of those feelings and waited for the other shoe to drop.

When he finally stopped laughing, he reached up and took off the universal translator he'd been wearing. "Don't let our appearance deceive you," he said in perfect Centauri. "We are more advanced than you believe. Come with me."

Garrick, Kiti and the rest of the landing party fell in behind Peligro and followed him to his village. They passed through a large town square surrounded on all sides by simple structures with thatched roofs. Peligro entered one and disappeared through the door.

Kiti was feeling a little apprehensive. They walked

down a hall, at the end of which was a door...a sliding door very similar to the doors on the *Dremel*. Too similar.

"We've been monitoring you since you entered our space. We did the same for Tybold's ship the *Tangipahoa*. Unfortunately for him, as soon as we found out the extent of his plans, his ship was rendered useless. At this point, Tybold has no idea that we control his ship. He can still come and go through the transporter, but he cannot leave orbit and he cannot fire his cannon."

Garrick reached for his comulator. "Don't bother Captain Marcus, if we had wanted to take control of your ship we could have. I wished to find out whether you were the same as Tybold. Had you proved deceitful, as he did, I might have destroyed your ship. I would have done his, but he may still prove useful, as he is currently staying and negotiating with the Nerutas."

"That's why you are neither allies nor enemies with either the Nerutas or the Otula. You're studying them." Kiti could barely contain her excitement. "This is where I wanted to come for my doctoral studies, but my grandmother refused and at the time, she was quite ill, so I never fulfilled that dream."

Peligro studied her for a moment. "Your grandmother raised you? Your mother's mother?"

"No, my father's mother."

"Interesting." Kiti watched Peligro stare at her, his eyes narrowed as he continued. "We have been here for more than one hundred years and we remain as neutral as possible. The entire Zolthor tribe is made up of my people and we have operatives within the other tribes. Tybold also was under observation but was never shown our knowledge. He has no idea that we are anything other than what we appear to be."

"What changed your mind about us? Why show us who you really are?" asked Garrick.

"Kitari Dolana, the sharmia, her rage toward Tybold is there on the surface for all to see, yet she remains polite. Controlled. Even or especially when she learned we had released him, she did not let her anger free. Being able to control oneself to the extent she did is one of the first signs of a civilized person.

"Tybold, though technologically advanced, was not civilized. When he found out we would not enter into negotiations with him, but would need to meet the head of your planet first, he flew into a rage."

Garrick said, "I can imagine he would have. Queen Dayanara would have had him arrested on the spot."

Kiti added, "I'm afraid I might have lost my civility, you see, he is the person behind my brother's murder."

"Ah," Peligro nodded in understanding. "That explains the rage I see cross your face at each mention of his name."

"If I was a man, I'd challenge him to a fight to the death, civilized or not."

"Easy Kiti, we'll capture him, "said Garrick. "And he *will* go back to face charges. As will Zia."

Peligro added, "They both must face charges here as

well, though not for murder. Before they fled to the Nerutas, they assaulted one of the women of my tribe. I cannot let that pass. We will have to come to an understanding before I can allow you to take them back to Centauri."

"Understood," agreed Garrick. "They must meet justice for their crimes on both our worlds."

They followed Peligro through the halls and corridors of a large building, most of which had to be underground and cloaked because their computer did not pick it up on the geographic scan.

"How do you do it?" Garrick finally asked.

"Yes," Kiti chimed in. "Why couldn't we see this? Our computer scan showed a large village, but none of the buildings were of this size."

"We have a cloaking device for the west and south portions of the planet. The device itself it at the south pole which is why the south looks barren. We actually have quite a thriving community there, maintaining the device."

"Ingenious," said Garrick. "But how did you get the other tribes to stay away, especially while you were building it. If nothing else my curiosity would've forced me to find out what was happening."

"They are much more interested in warring with each other than exploring new territory. Old legends about a monster haunting the area might have helped some."

As they continued to walk, Kiti observed the tall

man in front of her. He reminded her of Joridan except for the height and of course the eyes. Joridan had the light blue, with white blond hair, the complete opposite of Kiti's green eyes and black hair. And although taller than Kiti, he'd been Garrick's height, not giant sized like Peligro.

Garrick interrupted Kiti's musing's with another question. "How long have you been here observing, I'm assuming that is your mission. You said more than one hundred years. How much more?"

"Correct. We've actually be on the planet for 121 years. I was born here as were my father and grandfather and great-grandfather before me. I will explain all to you at dinner, assuming you will join us. I've had accommodations prepared. It's going to take more than a few hours to formulate our plans."

Kiti was shown to her room. It was sumptuous. That was the only way to describe it. There was a sitting room with couch, a two person snuggler, and a couple of chairs surrounding a small oval serving table. She could picture serving drinks and visiting with Garrick and all their friends in this room.

There was a real bed in the bedroom. Not the wall bed like on the ship, but a real bed with a tall, over-stuffed mattress and a canopy. Even Audra's bed in the palace didn't have a canopy.

Kiti felt like a princess. She felt spoiled and pampered. It was a nice feeling. Almost as nice as being courted by Garrick.

Laid out on the bed was a beautiful outfit with a note. *Please wear this to dinner with my compliments – P*

It was a long skirt and short vest that laced up the front. The skirt was cut full and slit up one side, so that her leg peeked out when she walked. The vest was very fitted and cut low enough to emphasize her bosom without being overtly sexy.

She decided it was more provocative than she thought when she entered Peligro's dining room and both Garrick and Peligro came to attention. Garrick frowned. Peligro smiled.

"You look lovely. I knew our traditional apparel would look spectacular on you." He said to Kiti while watching for Garrick's reaction.

The man was ornery as hell. He was trying to force a confrontation with Garrick. And from the look on Garrick's face he was succeeding.

Kiti steered the conversation in another direction. "How are we going to capture Tybold, especially if he has the Nerutas to do his bidding? And what part is Zia playing in this? She is power hungry and will be with Tybold only as long as he is powerful. As soon as he loses that, she will move on to someone else and we may never get her."

"I have *very* trustworthy spies among the Nerutas. They tell me that Tybold has bought as much kalcion as was available for sale. Zia has been seen leaving the headquarters of the Nerutas Talmud, Sunev. We believe she is attempting to trade her sexual favors for kalcion."

"I wonder how Tybold will pay for the metal. He cannot possess much in the way of beras, which I believe is the Procon currency," said Garrick. "But he could have jewels that we're not aware of or, most likely, he is trading technology. He has access to all of Centauri's technology from the *Tangipahoa*. The Nerutas will probably use it to attack the Otula first. It will be a massacre."

Peligro shook his head. "First, there is another traders market tomorrow in Sepiwa, the Nerutas capital city. We'll attend the market and capture Tybold when he proves he cannot pay for the kalcion he has already purchased. The Nerutas will be more than willing to hand him over, if they don't kill him first. Hopefully, by that time we will have the results back from the crime scene that will prove that Zia was the person who committed the assault.

"Second, the fight would likely *not* be a massacre. The kalcion swords we use are impervious to your blasters. Believe me. We've tried to destroy them. Unlike the raw metal, which is pliable or it couldn't be made into swords, there is a change that happens to the metal in the sword making process. It renders it impervious to most advanced weapon fire."

"Swords are no match for blasters, no matter how strong the metal," argued Garrick.

Peligro smiled. "Let's test it shall we? I do request

that you put your weapon on stun, just in case I'm not as quick as I used to be."

"I don't think this is a good idea," protested Kiti. "What happens if you're wrong and Garrick does stun you? It could cause an interplanetary incident, over a silly demonstration."

"It will be all right, Kitari Dolana. I give you my word that there will be no repercussions should your captain manage to stun me." He turned to Garrick. "Shall we begin?"

"With pleasure." Garrick replied, checking his blaster to make sure it was on stun and then fired without warning.

Peligro blocked easily, again and again. It didn't matter how fast Garrick fired or where he aimed it was blocked.

Finally, Kiti shouted, "Enough, the point has been made."

Garrick holstered his blaster and Peligro sheathed his sword. Both men returned to the table and after they sat down, Kiti told them, "After seeing that demonstration, I know what Tybold is going to do with the kalcion he's buying." They both looked at her expectantly. "He's going to use it to shield his ship."

"He couldn't have bought enough to shield a starship. The amount needed would be massive." Garrick said.

"It doesn't have to be very thick. Only the thickness of a sword." Kiti replied.

Garrick nodded, understanding for the first time. "Then he can attack any starship he comes across with impunity," Garrick theorized. "Our weapons are useless against this metal. They'll be able to fire on the other starships until their shields fail, then board and take what they will. Pirates! We rid our world of pirates long ago but now...they will be undefeatable."

"But how will he build the shield without returning to Centauri?" asked Kiti.

Peligro answered that question. "The Nerutas are skilled metal smiths. They are well known for their swords, the best on Procon. Building shields for a star-ship would not be difficult for them."

Garrick took a drink of the wine served with their dinner. He paced the room taking a drink at each end. Kiti knew he did some of his best thinking when he paced like this. She just wasn't sure the wine would help the process any. "We have to find a way to" she help up her index finger, "one--stop the construction of the shield, two—capture Tybold, three—apprehend Zia before she convinces Sunev to pick up where Tybold leaves off.

"The woman may be the most dangerous of the three. Tybold and Sunev are predictable but the woman...she desires power and will go to whatever lengths necessary to get it," stated Peligro.

"Even to trying her wiles on the other tribal Talmuds. I would start with the Otula and move on till she reaches you." Kiti said pointedly to Peligro. "Again."

Peligro chuckled. "Leave it to a woman to know the ways of another woman."

"It has nothing to do with being a woman," Kiti retorted. "She took my Princess and friend from me once. I won't underestimate her again."

For security purposes, they adjourned to Peligro's private living quarters to conclude their plans. His quarters consisted of one large room, similar to hers on the ship in functionality, with eating, sitting and sleeping space all in the same room. That was where the similarities stopped. He had the largest, most imposing bed she'd ever seen angled in one corner of the room. She supposed if she was seven feet tall she'd need a big bed too. Admittedly, she thought of sharing that big bed with Peligro. He was absolutely the most beautiful man she'd ever seen. Yet, something was lacking. Feelings. She had no feelings for him. Whereas, thoughts of sharing that bed with Garrick gave her hot flashes. She sat down in the chair farthest away from the bed, afraid if she sat near it would call to her.

She was trying to keep up with their conversation, but that damn bed. It did things to her. Made her imagination run wild, picturing herself atop Garrick, him pumping into her from the rear, her sitting in his lap and leaning back till his cock hit her vagina just right and she exploded in ecstasy. Krios, the fun they could have in a bed like this one.

As she felt the flush rise up her cheeks, she turned her head quickly from staring at the bed. Garrick must have seen because he suddenly said, "I believe that we will take advantage of your hospitality for the night. It's late and we still have a lot to do before tomorrow. I'll contact the ship and have fresh uniforms sent down."

"That won't be necessary. For what I have in mind you will need local Nerutas garb." Peligro said. "You'll need to disguise yourselves in case you come in contact with Tybold or Zia. Neither of them know you well and though they may have met you, they will be expecting you to be the Captain and Tensign they have met."

"Agreed. What is our cover story to be?" she asked. She took a sip of her wine and watched Garrick, who had a distinctly predatory look on his face.

"You are to be a kalcion trader and his mistress, of course."

Kiti choked on her wine. "His what?"

Peligro continued, "This will give you access to the kalcion sellers and attract Sunev like a magnet. His belief is that a mistress is fair game."

"What? As opposed to a wife? It would never occur to him that a mistress could be a..a wife-in-waiting?"

"No, it would not. For him a mistress is someone who can be bought or in some cases stolen."

"Then Kiti won't go," said Garrick.

"Garrick, don't be ridiculous. Of course, I'll go. If I get stolen or you sell me—"

"That will never happen."

"—we'll be that much closer to Tybold and Zia. They're probably staying with Sunev. Isn't that right, Peligro?"

"Not according to our sources. They have rented a house close to Sunev's headquarters. That's the reason we've been able to see Zia come and go. I don't understand how Tybold can't know what she's doing, but perhaps he does and that is part of his plan." Peligro ventured.

"Unlikely," said Garrick. "From what I know of Tybold he is not inclined to share what he believes is his, including his women."

Kiti had been sitting too long. She got up and stretched her hands over her head then bent backwards to stretch her back. All conversation ceased as the two men suddenly became transfixed watching her. When she straightened back up she realized one of her breasts had escaped the silky material.

She turned quickly away and readjusted the short top, swearing she'd blushed more tonight than ever in her life. She had to get out of here and calm herself away from these two. "If you gentlemen will excuse me, I need some air." She turned and left, not waiting to see if they responded or not.

Garrick tried to follow but Peligro stopped him. "My friend, leave her be. She needs some time to get over her embarrassment. She will return and all will be well. Trust me."

$\mathcal{K}$iti did return. But by the time she did Peligro had taken his leave and Garrick was pacing.

"You needn't have waited up for me." Kiti said when she entered the room.

"As if I had a choice," he said wrapping her in his arms the moment he reached her.

She went willingly into his embrace. "I was embarrassed. It's not every day I have a boob fall out of my clothing."

"I know but I couldn't take my eyes off of you, unfortunately neither could our host." Garrick frowned and hugged her tighter to him.

It was too easy. Teasing him. And totally irresistible. "Couldn't take his eyes off me, huh? Well, he is a very attractive man." Garrick's hold on her tightened. "A woman would have to be blind not to notice..." his hold now was so tight she almost couldn't breathe. "Okay, okay, I'll quit." She laughed.

Sensing that he needed reassurance she caressed his face. "You know I'm a one man woman. You've nothing to worry about, Sweetheart." She stopped short of saying I love you. It was too soon to be sure. They had explosive sex but was there love? They were friends and that could build into love, but had it already? Was that why she'd not been devastated when she and Anton drifted apart?

She'd known that Anton searched for his lifemate and attributed their lack of intimacy to that, but she was as much to blame as he was. Even before Darius and Audra's happiness became the standard she wanted to achieve, she'd ached for more than Anton could give her.

Garrick had always attracted her but she and Anton had been paired for what seemed like forever. While they enjoyed each other both knew it was not permanent. Anton had a lifemate and they both knew that Kiti was not that person. Did she have a lifemate? She didn't know much about her family on her mother's side. Her parents had been killed in a lab accident when she was three and Joridan was one. For as long as she could remember there'd only been the three of them. Her grandmother, her and Joridan. He'd been her best friend and his death had taken a piece of her heart, her soul.

Raised by her paternal grandmother, her mother was never mentioned. Whether from dislike or just lack of knowledge, Kiti didn't know. She did know that her parents had married without her grandmother's approval but all seemed to be forgiven and her grandmother never ceased tiring of telling her how much she looked like her father and grandfather before him, with her clear dark green eyes and black hair. She admitted they were distinctive. She couldn't remember seeing anyone with eyes the color of hers. Not that she paid that much attention, but she thought she would have noticed if anyone had eyes a clear jewel green like hers.

Joridan didn't have them. He had light blue eyes and blond hair. Her grandmother didn't have them. Her eyes were blue and her hair was white and had been as long as Kiti could remember.

Since her grandfather died before she was born, she only had her grandmothers memories to rely on. She didn't even know what her parents looked like. There were no pictures of them that she'd ever found. She'd gone through all of her grandmother's things when she'd died. There were pictures of the three of them from the time that Joridan was two and she was not quite four but nothing prior to that. It was like she didn't exist before then.

These feelings she had for Garrick were bringing out all kinds of questions about her heritage. She was a historian and anthropologist for goodness sake and she'd never thought to research her own family.

Kiti cuddled up to Garrick who'd fallen asleep after their exertions. Too many questions and not enough answers. Now, though, was not the time to begin searching for answers about her family. Tomorrow was a busy day.

Tomorrow they would begin their plan to capture Tybold.

Kiti put on the clothes that Peligro provided. She was beginning to think the man was a sex fiend. Both outfits he'd given her were very sexy. This one was a short tight skirt, knee high boots, a knife strapped to her thigh and completing the ensemble, a white shirt with long blousy sleeves and low cut neckline. She felt like a character out of a book the whole *Dremel* crew had read when studying English and Earth on the trip to get Audra. The book was called Treasure Island.

"Wow!" Garrick whistled. "You look spectacular."

"Thanks, but I know you. You're having visions of playing pirate and wench tonight, aren't you?"

Garrick didn't speak for the longest time, just stared at her like he'd never seen her before.

"Wheebee got your tongue?" she said finally.

"Hmm." He shook his head. "Sorry, my mind just went all kinds of places it shouldn't go. I must admit I like the way the Proconian women dress."

"You, my dear, are a closet anthropologist. Admit it. You are as fascinated by these people as I am. Hey, you look pretty good yourself."

Good?! Her mouth watered and she nearly came when she saw him. He wore a leather vest and skin tight pants, no shirt and a wide leather belt. His knee high boots had built in knife sheaths on the outside.

The vest emphasized Garrick's muscular arms. Arms she was very familiar with. Arms that comforted her when she cried because she missed her brother, arms that held her aloft when she rode him during sex. Strong arms. Good arms.

Her mind returned along with a question. "How are we going to keep Tybold and Zia from recognizing us especially with all this skin hanging out?"

It was Peligro who responded from her doorway. "He will be looking for the Dragonera Captain and Tensign if he is looking for you at all. He will not look twice at Grold and Isabo of the Htrae. We should be fine as long as you don't get too close and spring the trap before we 're ready to close it."

"You don't think he'll find it odd when he sees a trader with his mistress in tow? I suppose he wouldn't since he has Zia. Hey, how about I'm the trader and Garrick is the mistress?"

Both men laughed at her jest.

"Seriously, are there so many traders that we will not be noticed?"

"She has a point. How big is this town and how many trader types will be there?" Garrick said.

Peligro motioned for them both to sit at the table in Kiti's room. Then he snapped his fingers and servants entered carrying trays laden with food and drink. "There is a lot to be said for the old ways of cooking and eating together."

Kiti closed her eyes and let the wonderful aromas wafting from the trays over take her senses. She smelled toasted bread, sweet honey and...coffee? "Garrick says the same thing. He always encourages his crew to take their meals in the common area together."

The servants put the trays on the table and Kiti was on them, her manners forgotten as her stomach rumbled. She smiled, grabbed a roll and took a large bite. "Mmm," was all that came out.

Garrick shook his head at her. "I've found you have to feed her before she's civilized in the mornings."

Kiti kicked him.

He laughed. "See what I mean? Anyway, I do find that eating together helps establish camaraderie and trust amongst the crew. You are far more likely to help someone you know, may even have become friends with than a stranger." Garrick grabbed a cup and poured himself some of the hot beverage. "What is this? It smells like coffee from Earth."

"It is. We've been on Earth longer than we've been on Procon. The Earthlings are not as advanced in some ways as the Proconian's. They are not ready for trade with advanced peoples they consider alien and a threat to their way of life.

"The Proconians have been trading since the first ships landed here hundreds of years ago. They have been offered all kinds of technology and have only accepted that which they needed at the time. As to weapons, they like close combat. When it was discovered that kalcion could be used to make swords and make them invulnerable to blasters… well there was then no option. Swords won out. They are more graceful and have many more uses than just killing.

"Earth's technology is more advanced than that of Procon, yet the Proconians are the more advanced people. It is an interesting dynamic." He turned his full attention toward Kiti. "I would love to discuss it with you at length."

Again Peligro watched Garrick for a reaction to his flirtation with Kiti.

"We would be happy to discuss Earthlings with you, though, our knowledge is limited. I doubt we would give you any insight to their behavior." Garrick responded.

Kiti was fed now and tired of watching these two butt heads over her, however flattering it might seem. "When do we leave?"

"Now, if you are both ready. You will attract Sunev like a bee to honey, to use an Earth phrase."

"What is a bee?" asked Garrick. "And what is honey? My familiarity with English from Earth is limited."

"I can answer that," said Kiti. "A bee is a flying insect. It goes from flower to flower, picking up pollen from one flower and distributing it to others as his collects it as well. Then it goes back to its hive and uses the pollen and vomit to build a structure called a comb where it lays it's larve. Honey is the sweet product produced by the pollen vomit combination.

"Earthlings value it and eat it because it is sweet and it also has healing properties. You've had it in one of Maggie's desserts," she said to Garrick. "Baklava." She smiled. "It's one of your favorites but I doubt you'd have eaten it had you known it contained vomit."

Garrick's look of disgust confirmed her assessment. "I don't think I'll eat that again."

"I'm sure we can find food just as disgusting at the kalcion trade show we'll be attending today." Peligro ventured.

"You're coming with us?" asked Kiti.

"Yes. I attend all the trade shows and it is not unusual for me to bring new traders with me. Though none have been as beautiful as you. Have I told you that you have the most beautiful green eyes? I've only seen them on one other person.

"Really? Who?"

"You will probably meet them today and I think it needs to be a surprise." Said Peligro cryptically.

***

Kiti spotted Zia right away and ducked behind a vendor's booth. She watched her meet a very handsome older man with long black hair, graying at the sides. He was dressed in a fashion similar to Garrick. She assumed he was Sunev or Zia wouldn't have been giving him the time of day. When Zia grabbed the man, kissed him and rubbed her body against his. Kiti knew she was right. This was Sunev.

She turned and pointed them out to Garrick who stood next to her scanning the area. When she turned back, Zia was gone and Sunev stared directly at her. She gulped. The man started toward her.

Kiti poked Garrick in the ribs with her elbow. "Here he comes. Shows on."

"I can see that." He moved slightly in front of Kiti, braced his legs apart and waited.

Sunev stopped in front of them,

"Sir?" Kiti said as she stared into her own green eyes. The same clear jewel green. The same up turn at the outer lid. "Why? Why didn't Peligro say anything? He had to know. But it's impossible. My father died when I was three. My grandmother told me over and over again, that my father was dead."

"What is your name, girl?" Demanded Sunev.

"Kitari Dolana of the planet Centauri."

"Kitari. It is a common name on Centauri?"

"No. My grandmother told me it is a family name, my father's—"

"Great grandmother's name." he finished for her.

Kiti wasn't sure she liked where this conversation was going. If it was true then Gram had lied to her all those years. "Yes. How? How can you know that?"

"Because if the tears in your eyes are any indication, you believe as I do, that I am your father."

Garrick stood and watched the emotions play across her face. Surprise, fear, disappointment, apprehension, and finally joy. "How can you be sure? How do we know you aren't saying these things just to take advantage of her?"

Sunev eyed Garrick. "You are her protector?"

"I am."

"Good. If you both will come with me to my home, I will show you. I can prove it to your and Kitari's satisfaction. Please."

Peligro appeared. "Do you believe me now, Father?"

Kiti and Garrick both whipped around to look at him. "Father?" They said in unison.

"You knew?" asked Kiti. "But you flirted with me, I thought..."

"As I wished you to think, sweet sister. I did not want you to put it together until you had met Father."

"You don't look anything like me or Sunev. How would I have put it together?" She stopped, approached Peligro and stared up into his eyes. Joridan's eyes.

"He and I had our mothers coloring. You were the only one that took after Father." Peligro said gently.

"Is she still alive? Was anything Gram told me the truth? Was she really my grandmother?"

"Kitari, you have many questions and I have some of my own. Please," Sunev took her hands in his, "please come home with me and together we will find the answers we seek."

"Garrick?" Kiti looked to him seeking reassurance and stability in her suddenly upside down world.

"This is important to you. To us. Let's go with him."

Kiti let go of Sunev's hands. Garrick hugged her to him. "We'll go get answers to your questions and then go after Tybold. He's not going anywhere. Peligro has control of his ship, remember?"

She nodded and grabbed his hand. She held it tight as they followed Sunev, with Peligro bringing up the rear. Excited, scared too, she wondered if anything about her life was true. How could Gram do this to her? How could Gram have raised her for more than twenty-five years on nothing but lies? If she hadn't been dead for the past seven years Kiti would have wrung her neck. Gram had always been adamant about telling the truth, yet it may turn out she was the biggest liar of all.

They entered a foyer with halls on either side. They took the hall on the right and went to the door at the end. Through the door was a small sitting room. Kiti thought this was their destination and waited for Sunev to ask them to sit. Instead he went to the far wall, waved his hand over a vase on the table and spoke some words at the picture above it that Kiti understood only some of. She remembered her grandmother telling her stories in that language or something very similar.

A door slid open where the picture had been. They all went through the door and entered another sitting room, this had only one picture on the wall, opposite the lone chair in the room. It was of a beautiful woman with long white blond hair and sky blue eyes. She was the female version of Peligro and obviously his mother. Still, Kiti saw nothing to convince her that Sunev was her father.

They finally entered another room covered in pictures. Family pictures.

Kiti gasped. There was a large family portrait in the middle of one wall. In it was Sunev holding a blond baby, a young Peligro standing next to his father, nearly as tall, and already too handsome for his own good.

The two of them stood behind two seated women. One was the beautiful woman in the other picture. She was holding a little girl, a toddler of about two, with black hair and vivid green eyes. Kiti. She recognized herself at that age from pictures of her, Joridan and their grandmother, who was the second woman in the picture.

Kiti turned to Sunev. "Why?" Tears streaked down her cheeks. She turned to Garrick, felt him wrap her in his protective arms. And she cried.

He said nothing. Just held her, kissing the top of her head.

None of them said anything. The only sounds were Kiti's sobs.

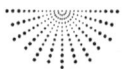

CHAPTER SEVEN

"You see my mother took you and your brother Joridan, when my wife died about a year after that portrait was done. It was at that time that I became Talmud of the Nerutas. We had worked for so long to that end. Mother said she wasn't going to let her grand babies grow up in that wicked environment.

"After Dolana died, I wasn't thinking clearly, my life had just ended you see. I know that sounds selfish and it was, but I was too bereft to think of anything except my loss. I certainly wasn't thinking about you and your brother, so I let Mother take you away."

"I'm named after your wife."

"Yes. It's ironic because to my knowledge my mother never liked Dolana, yet she gave you that name. Because of it your mother has always been a part of you."

"Why did she not take Peligro, too?

"I was nearly grown." Peligro answered. "At the time of our mother's death, I was ten and had already begun my training to become Talmud of the Zolthor."

"Our intel said that the Talmudship has been in your family for more than one hundred years. It was obviously wrong, since Sunev did not become Talmud of the Zolthor."

"No. It's correct. I took it from my grandfather. To be honest I don't think anyone else wanted it. Too much paperwork." He whispered conspiratorially.

"Kiti," Sunev interrupted. "I know you have a million questions but I have two that will not wait. The first is for Garrick."

Kiti didn't like where this was going. "Can't we start with number two first?"

Garrick silenced her with one look.

"Fine. Ask you question." said Kiti.

Sunev continued. "Garrick, Captain of the **Dremel**, do you intend to marry my daughter? We are more conservative here on Procon than on Centauri. If a man is sleeping with one woman on a regular basis, she is one of three things: his wife, his mistress or his fiancée."

Garrick didn't even hesitate. "Yes sir, I do intend to marry her."

Kiti jumped up. "You can't be serious. Don't tell him that."

"Of course, I'm serious. Why do you think I sent all

the flowers to you, I was courting you. Why do you think I rearranged my schedule every day so I could have lunch with you? I tried to have dinner with you every night but was unable to arrange it. Did you think I did it just because we're friends? Kiti?

"I don't know what I thought. But I do know that I'm not going to be forced into any decision right now, this minute."

"That's fine," said Sunev with a wink at Garrick. "My second question is who killed your brother?"

"Tybold. Or at least he's the one who arranged for the ambush in which Joridan was killed. I need to have him pay for what he did. I can't think of anything else, until Joridan's murderer is brought to justice. Not love or marriage or parentage. Can you understand?"

"Of course. I understand totally. It took many years but I finally brought the killers of your mother to justice. She was killed in a lab accident, but it was a planned accident. She was working on a new formula for kalcion treatment. It would have meant millions to the manufacturer. As it turned out, the formula didn't work, but it was too late for my Dolana."

Kiti nodded in understanding. "Murderers don't care if formulas work or if the information their masters wanted is retrieved. They kill." She leapt from the snuggler, leaving Garrick grasping at air when he tried to stop her. She was shouting now, her rage overtaking her. "They kill. That's all they do. Tybold wants power. He thought he could get it through Slavarien and Joridan was killed in the ambush Tybold arranged. That makes him a murderer. Just because he didn't do the deed himself, doesn't make him any less guilty."

Garrick went to her, held her at arms length by the shoulders. "Kiti. I know how you feel. Joridan was my friend, too. But you can't let the rage overcome you. We'll lose him and any advantage we have, if you do. You know this."

Kiti took several cleansing breaths. In and out. In and out. Breathe. "Okay, I'm better now. I won't lose control again."

He hugged her to him. "Sweetheart, I know you won't. You've been amazing. I'm not sure I could remain as controlled as you are, if it had been my brother, Carstin, who'd died."

"I could have him arrested and killed now, but that would not serve justice for either of us. He must be made to pay for not only Joridan's murder but for all the other men and women that were killed that day." Sunev said. "Peligro tells me that you have a plan to catch him in the act. We will be able to arrest him, legally, for fraud and you will be able, again, legally to file for extradition to Centauri to face trial for murder."

"We may be able to fool Tybold, he's never paid much attention to those under him, but Zia has met me and talked to me, when she kidnapped our queen. How will we fool her?"

"Easy. You will simply be my daughter, in from the out country colony of Golong province. Garrick will be your husband. I cannot have my daughter being the mistress of a trader. Peligro will get you the appropriate clothing as befits the daughter of the Talmud of the Nerutas."

"I shall return," said Peligro as he left the room.

Sunev went to the side bar and poured the three of them glasses of a local wine. "It is from the Dolana winery," he said proudly handing each of them a glass.

"Thank you," said Kiti and Garrick.

Peligro returned with the clothing and with a woman by his side. "This is Melana, my wife."

"Your wife? This is just getting too strange," Kiti said taking a big gulp of her wine.

"I know he had you thinking that he was an unmarried man. It is prudent for business purposes that some traders think that. As long as he comes to my bed each night, he can flirt all he wants."

"Now you see why I love her." Peligro looked at his wife and Kiti saw that same look that Darius had when he looked at Audra.

"Hmpft." Melana said handing the clothing to Kiti. "He loves to flirt. He would run like a scared child if anyone took him up on his flirtations. He knows I would kill him."

The clothing she gave her was a long skirt, similar to the one she'd worn the previous night and the one the Melana had on now. The blouse did not change, but there was a low slung belt with a knife in a scabbard. Meant to be used by a right handed person, the scabbard was worn on the left side of the body. There was also a heavy jeweled collar that Melana gave to Kiti.

"This belonged to your mother. Now that you are back, I think you should wear it."

Kiti looked from the collar to the family picture on the wall. There was her mother wearing the same collar. The bib hung to mid breast and jewels of every color adorned it. It basically covered all the skin left bare by the blouse.

She loved it.

"I'll wear it proudly. Although when Zia sees this, she's liable to kill me just for the collar, not caring who I am."

"Not while I'm around," said Garrick and Sunev together.

Kiti laughed. "I've gotten three outfits, a father, brother and sister all in one night. That has got to be a record." Had it only been one night? It seemed like it'd been weeks since they'd landed, so much had happened.

The five of them left for the trader market. Garrick and Kiti were now going as Sunev's daughter and son-in-law, traders from the out country. The advantage of this was twofold. Tybold and Zia had both already met Sunev and were negotiating with him. When they meet Garrick and Kiti, even if they do recognize them, Sunev will be there to assure them that they are none other than his daughter and her husband. Kiti's amazing resemblance to her father will quash any doubts.

Sunev went over the plan. "I will recommend

Garrick's kalcion product as the best buy. Tybold will agree to purchase it. Contracts will be drawn and eventually Tybold will try to leave with the kalcion and no payment. It is at this point that he will be arrested by Peligro's people for the assault committed on Melana."

"What? Melana was assaulted?" Garrick's hands formed to fists.

Kiti said, "It had to be Zia, Tybold has never been known for physical violence against women. Zia on the other hand, I believe to be capable of it without thought."

Peligro's anger was there, but controlled. "She was attacked when she entered our living quarters. Not the one that you saw but the one that we show to visitors. Melana did not see her face, only that it was someone smaller than herself. As you see, my Melana is not a small woman. She was not grievously injured, but it should never have happened." He hit the wall with his fist. Kiti was surprised it didn't go right through.

"Calm yourself, my love. I am not injured any longer." Melana took his hand and kissed his knuckles, now abraded from hitting the wall

He continued, "Zia was the only female visitor at the time. She and Tybold left Zolthor land the next day."

"Why, if they were going to leave anyway, would she have attacked Melana? What was she looking for?" asked Garrick.

"She'd been attempting to lure me to her bed, or more specifically, get into mine. We thought it was simply getting caught in our private quarters that caused her to attack. You think differently, Garrick?"

"Yes. There's definitely more to this than meets the eye. I believe she was looking for money or perhaps maps to a kalcion mine. Anything they could use to trade for the kalcion or get it on their own."

"That's true," said Kiti. "Zia isn't the type to get ruffled by getting caught trying to sleep with someone's husband. That's just business as usual for her. Getting caught stealing would be totally different. It would bring unwanted attention by the authorities."

"Was there any mention of money or anything such as that?" asked Garrick.

"We had talked about the mines that the Zolthor control. Kalcion mines. Many of them are not operational now. It became too dangerous to continue to mine them, so they have been closed."

"Do you have maps to these mines?"

"They are all on computer."

"But Zia wouldn't have known that," Kiti interjected. "She thought you were as backward as you appeared. Uh, you know what I mean." She was embarrassed she'd thought them backward, when they were most definitely not and were probably more advanced technologically than her people were. Although, now she didn't know who her people were. Was she Centaurian or Zolthorian?

Peligro smiled. "Don't be embarrassed Kiti. You

believed what you saw with your eyes. That's what we desire for everyone to see."

"So we can be sure she didn't get anything, but there is another thing we are now sure of," said Garrick.

"What is that?" asked Sunev.

"We're sure they can't pay for the kalcion they're ordering. If they could, Zia wouldn't have been looking for maps to mines."

Everyone in the room nodded in agreement. "It will make them more desperate to get the orders in and loaded as soon as possible, so they can make an escape before the bills come due."

"We need to get them off guard. If they get too nervous, they'll try to flee and it's possible that if they can't use their starship, they'll steal another. I'm going to have the **Dremel** change orbit so it is on the opposite side of your moon and out of sight, so to speak. We have thus far remained out of sensor range and I would keep it that way."

"In the mean time," Sunev added, "I can make it known that I will guarantee Tybold's purchases. Zia will think her wily ways have been successful."

"Okay, then," said Kiti. "Let's go make this happen."

CHAPTER EIGHT

*T*he market was crowded. Vendors sold jewelry, swords, food, and clothes. Anything and everything that could be sold, was for sale. There were dozens of kalcion miners and mine owners, as well, selling everything from the raw ore to highly milled and polished nuggets suitable for jewelry.

Kiti noted there were few women dressed as she and Melana were. As wives. Peligro hadn't been exaggerating when he said she would fit right in dressed as a mistress. There had to be a hundred women wearing the short skirt and boots like those he'd given her that morning. She was pleased to see that the sexy women seemed to have no effect on Garrick or Peligro. Both men were being very protective of her and Melana.

Sunev led their little group to a stall right in the middle of the large convention center where this event was being held.

"Santro! My friend." He clapped a large man with dark red hair on the back.

"Sunev! You get uglier every year. Soon the children will run from you in terror."

Both men laughed. "Santro. I would have you know my daughter, Kitari and her husband, Garrick. They are traders from the Golong province here for the market."

The men shook hands.

Kiti stared. She couldn't help it. Santro had the darkest auburn hair she'd ever seen. More black than brown, but with definite red tones, worn tied back with a leather thong.. His left eye was the color of early spring moss. The right eye was covered with a black leather patch. A long crescent shaped scar went from his right eye to his chin. The man was extremely handsome still and without the scar would have been devastating. "It is very nice to meet a friend of my family."

Santro took Kiti's hand and gave it the lightest of kisses. "I am so happy to finally meet you. Of course, I would have known you anywhere. With those eyes, there is only one man who could be your father." He eyed Kiti up and down, "Luckily for us, the rest of you takes after sweet Dolana."

"You knew my mother?"

"Yes, for many years. I have known your parents since I was a boy. Peligro and I trained together and I fostered with your family."

"I'm sorry. I've been away for a long time. What kind of training?

"Sword training. Your father is the second greatest swordsman on the planet."

"And who is the greatest swordsman?"

"Why, I am, of course." Santro laughed loud and long at his jest.

Kiti looked at Sunev. "Can you teach me, Father? I would love to learn how to use a sword."

"I'm surprised he has not already taught you.?

"I wasn't raised here. After Mother died, my little brother and I went to live with my grandmother."

"I see." Santro glanced at Sunev for confirmation.

"You must remember the condition I was in after Dolana died. I sent all my children away. Peligro went to and was fostered by, Hardok of the Zolthor, my father. The little ones, Kitari and Joridan, went with my mother."

"I remember you were in no condition to raise children. It was many years before you were capable of caring for yourself. Kitari, if you need my services or assistance in any way, you have but to call me."

Kiti nodded. "Santro that is very kind of you. If I have need I will definitely take you up on your offer. Thank you."

"So where is Joridan? Did he come with you on this trip?"

"My brother was murdered. The man responsible is here."

"You are going after him." Santro stated the obvious.

"We are going to arrest him," interjected Garrick, "and take him back to Centauri for trial. Both him and his companion, Zia"

"Ah, Zia. I know her." He winked at Garrick. One of those man to man winks, meaning he knew her in the carnal sense.

Sunev laughed. "Every man here may 'know' her, she has not been stingy with her charms."

"Nor has she been unclear about her desire to trade those charms for kalcion," said Santro. "She wanted me to sell her, and someone named Tybold, all that I have. I said I would love to, for a price that didn't include her various charms. She was rather upset with me."

"We would like to ask you to help her find us." said Garrick. "Tell her you will send her to a new trader with the cheapest price. We need to get Tybold out in the open. No one has seen him since they came to this land. The dwelling has been under surveillance but I want our case against them to be ironclad, not only for Centauri justice but for Proconian justice as well."

"The results of the tests on the evidence gathered after Melana was attacked will not be completed for several days," said Peligro.

"Stop! What is this about Melana being attacked?" asked Santro.

"She was assaulted in our sleeping quarters. Attacked with a vase. They cracked over her head as she entered the room." Peligro wrapped his arm around Melana's waist and brought her close to him.

Kiti smiled at her newly found brother. His protectiveness of his wife reminded her of Joridan. Though he'd been the younger of the two of them, he always tried to protect her. When Kiti started going out with Anton Coridian, he followed them. He popped up anytime he thought Anton was being too familiar with Kiti. It was months before Joridan finally let them go on a date without him and a year before he told Anton, it was okay for him to be dating Kiti.

Krios! It seemed like yesterday she'd told him about her assignment to retrieve the princess. He was starting his tour of duty in the elite Dragonera squad directly under the command of Anton. He was excited and proud.

She didn't know it would be the last time she'd see him. She didn't know she wouldn't get the chance to tell him again how much she loved him, to have him hold her in his arms and tell her everything would be okay when she and Anton had a fight. She didn't know. Then Tybold and Slavarien took him away forever. She would never get the chance to tell him any of those things she took for granted. He was not supposed to die before she did. It just wasn't supposed to happen that way.

Santro's voice brought her back from the memories. "Melana, are you all right? Were you injured?"

"I'm fine. I had a huge lump on my head where the vase hit but nothing else."

"Are you sure it was a woman that hit you? Could it have been a man? Didn't you say that Tybold has not been seen since the first night he arrived on Nerutas land?"

"He would have to be a small man. I suppose that Tybold would fit that description." She turned to Peligro. "Now we have an even greater reason to wait for the results of the test on the vase to come back. We may be chasing the wrong person."

"If that is the case," said Garrick, " then perhaps, Santro can convince Zia, that Tybold is the wrong player to back in this standoff."

"Ah," said Kiti. "Divide and conquer. Get Zia to turn on Tybold. She will then give him to us in order to rid herself of him. But how do we do that? What can we offer her that would be better than queen? There I'm assuming that Tybold plans on returning to Centauri and attempting to take over the throne."

"That would be reckless even for Tybold. He will only have one ship."

"But that ship will be invincible because of the kalcion shields," said Kiti.

"Everything and everyone has a weakness. We will have to find the *Tangipahoa's* and exploit it."

Sunev interrupted Kiti and Garrick. "Listen to yourselves. You're giving up even before we start. I can guarantee that neither of these people will leave this planet alive."

"No, Sunev, you cannot kill them." Kiti touched her father's arm. "They must go back to Centauri for trial and punishment. There are many more families than ours that need closure on this. That had their loved ones killed in that ambush."

"You are a kind woman Kitari. I would not be so accommodating to anyone else, but you are my daughter and I will agree to your requests. I will have my vengeance on these two for their crimes. Joridan's murder and Melana's assault will not go unpunished."

"I understand and I thank you. Now what?"

"Well," Garrick answered. "We need to stick with the plan. Zia will be back to try another deal with Santro. He'll agree this time to help her by sending her to us. We will know then if Kiti and I are recognized. If we are Zia and Tybold will attempt to leave the planet. If we are not then we will agree to sell them the kalcion they want. Either way we will get Tybold back out into the open where he can be arrested."

"Whether, in the open or at his accommodations, we'll still need a warrant and an extradition treaty to get them to Centauri. As much as I might want to, I don't make the law. I just uphold it," said Sunev. "When I must."

"I'm glad," said Kiti. "I wouldn't want my father to have this evil blood on his hands. I don't want us to get down to Tybold's level. Joridan would not want that."

"After this is done, I would like to hear about my son."

"You'd have been proud of him. He was a gentle warrior."

"I'm glad to know this. Ah, " said Sunev, "here

comes Zia. Keep your back to her Kiti. I want to see her reaction when I introduce you. Peligro and Melana, leave before she sees you. She won't come over if she sees you here. At this point I don't think she has seen anyone but Santro and me."

He went forward to intercept her, allowing Peligro and Melana to slip into the crowd.

"Zia, my beauty. I want you to meet my daughter Kiti and her husband Garrick. They are kalcion traders from Golong province."

Zia turned toward Kiti and stopped. Her eyes widened just a bit, then she said, "You look just like your father with those dancing green eyes. Until Sunev, I'd never seen eyes like yours before. Oh, where are my manners?" She held out her hand. "I'm Zia. Very glad to meet you."

"And I you, Zia. My father has told me much about you. You've made quite the impression." Kiti said as she shook Zia's hand.

"Odd, he never mentioned you to me."

"Probably because we have not been able to visit in a very long time. Garrick and I have been developing our mine. It's not been an easy task, but it's been worth it. Now we're here to sell our kalcion."

"Really? I may have a buyer for you."

"That's kind of you Zia, but it appears there are many buyers here. We must get the best price possible."

"I can guarantee my friend's will be the best price, if you have enough of the ore."

"What can your friend offer? What price?" asked Garrick.

"He will pay five percent above market, currently 2500 beras per ton," answered Zia, "if you have more than one million tons."

"Why was I not offered that?" asked Santro, a bit incensed. "The deal you gave me was ten percent under market."

"Well," said Zia as she sashayed over to Santro. There were other benefits included in your deal." She stroked his chin and winked at him. "I can't very well offer those same benefits to Kitari and Garrick, now can I?"

"Hmph," snorted Santro. "Your charms, nice as they are, are not worth ten percent."

Zia lifted her chin and walked back to Kiti and Garrick.

Garrick tried to smooth things over. "We'll talk it over tonight and give you our answer tomorrow. If we agree, we expect to meet your friend."

"Of course. That shouldn't be a problem. He's been feeling a little ill lately, but I'm sure he's much better now."

"Glad to hear it. Shall we meet here at the noon hour? I have a feeling our response will be a positive one. We can formalize our agreement over a meal and some wine." Garrick added.

"Good. Tybold will be happy to hear it. He is anxious to leave this planet and return home."

"Oh, where are you from?" asked Kiti.

"We came here from Delaz." Zia answered avoiding the question.

"I'm not familiar with Delaz," lied Kiti. "Garrick and I were both raised on Procon."

"You haven't missed anything. Delaz is a backwater planet run by a vicious tyrant." Zia spit on the ground and rubbed it in with her toe. "That is what I think of all Slavariens."

"Well," said Kiti, "I can tell you really don't like them whoever the Slavariens are."

"They are the ones who rule Delaz," said Zia. "One of them nearly beat me to death. My Lord Tybold saved me from them."

That explains a lot, thought Kiti, but she said, "Well then you must be very grateful to Lord Tybold."

"Oh, I am. I would do just about anything for him short of murder."

The part about Delaz and the Slavariens at least was true. Ranzon and his father King Thoriz were vicious, evil men. Thoriz was in prison on Centauri and Ranzon was dead. Killed by Lara, now Queen of Delaz. She and her husband, Anton, were king and queen at the behest of the Delazin people. They were bringing the Delazin people into the current century with new infrastructure and technology.

The people, most of whom were former slaves, were learning how to govern themselves, to respect themselves, communicate with other cultures. All the things that Kiti took for granted.

Anyone who knew anything about Delaz and the nation building happening there now, wouldn't think twice about someone one from there buying large quantities of kalcion.

The question still was how Tybold would pay for it. That question was soon answered, when a bank in the Otula territory was robbed. A single man, armed with a blaster and photon grenades, walked in, demanded all the money and simply disappeared into thin air.

Santro was sure it was Tybold that robbed his people. "He seems to be racking up more crimes with which to be charged. Assault, fraud, murder and now theft. Those are just the ones we know about. I'm sure there are many more we are unaware of."

That night Kiti and Garrick stayed with Sunev. Kiti regaled him with stories of Joridan as a boy and as a man. Sunev in turn told her about her mother, Dolana.

Kiti was more complete, more content than she'd ever been. She had a family. A father, brother and sister-in-law. She'd also make sure that Garrick didn't have to marry into her family. Having sex was one thing. Marriage was something else altogether. Marriage was forever. There was no way, she was marrying at the end of a blaster.

CHAPTER NINE

hat wasn't love. Kiti wanted love. The all consuming kind of love she saw between Audra and Darius and Anton and Lara. The kind of love her parents had. The same kind she finally realized she had for Garrick.

It had taken her time to come to that conclusion. She'd been with Anton so long; she hadn't recognized real love when it hit her square between the eyes. It was lust, only lust she told herself. She believed it for a long time, until she realized she wanted to be with him even when they weren't having sex. She loved the scent of him, looked forward to seeing him when they'd been apart, even if only for a short while.

She realized he'd been courting her but thought it was just to get into her bed. At least that's what she believed until they'd met Sunev. Then Garrick said he'd marry her. Only the stress of the moment and Sunev's big sword brought that about, decided Kiti. After all, what was he supposed to say, 'No, I don't want to marry her, I'm just fucking her for now.' That would've gone over real well.

Well, Garrick needn't worry about her. She had family again now. Losing Anton wasn't devastating and she was learning to live without Joridan. It wasn't easy, she missed him terribly, but every day she remembered something good about him and about their life together. Every day she made a little more progress. Every day she thought about what he would want for her and tried to do that, not concentrate on how much she missed him. She decided to think of it as he was on a long vacation and she'd see him when he returned, rather than he was dead. It made it easier to get by each day without him. Someone who's never been that close to a sibling can't understand her pain. They don't know what it's like to lose a piece of yourself and she hoped they never found out.

Soon she would get justice. Tybold and Zia would be in prison. She'd move to Procon then. Have Sunev teach her the way of the sword, she could teach history and anthropology in one of the schools, learn her own history.

Or maybe she'd just visit. It would be hard to leave her friends, really they were her family now. Sunev and Peligro may be family by blood but the people she loved were on Centauri, her family by choice.

"**W**ell?" asked Tybold when Zia returned. "Did you find a deal for us?"

"I believe so. With Sunev's daughter and her husband."

"We didn't meet any daughter."

"They're here for the market. They live in Golong province and this is their first market. Apparently they've spent most of the last few years working and building their mine. There was something familiar about her, but I think it's just because she has her father's amazing green eyes. They are so unique."

"Unique green eyes. Yes, I remember. But I've seen another with those eyes, if I could just remember who. Oh well it will come to me. What price did you offer?"

"Five percent over market, just as you told me to do. But how are we going to pay that. I don't even know how we will pay for these accommodations. We should have stayed on the Tangipahoa and just transported down as needed," complained Zia.

"We needed to be here. How can you work your magic, my love, if you are on the ship?"

"Well," Zia answered mollified by his praise. "I suppose I couldn't. I still think I could have gotten Santro to agree to my deal."

"I'm just as glad he didn't. I don't like to share you. Now come work your magic on me."

"Of course." She smiled, took his hand and led him to their bedroom.

*D*awn couldn't come soon enough for Kiti, she'd barely slept. She and Sunev talked into the wee hours of the morning. Regaling each other with stories of lost loved ones.

Kiti spoke of Joridan and remembered who he *really* was for the first time since the funeral. "He was so strong. Not just his body but his mind too. I leaned on him so much. Depended on him to be there for Gram, when she refused further treatment by the med-techs. She said she was tired. Her mind was tired and she didn't want to prolong the inevitable any longer.

"I don't blame her. There are days I'm so tired I don't think I can stand it another day, but then I wake up and I'm refreshed and ready to take on the world. I can't imagine waking up every day as tired as I was the day before. I would be depressed. That's what Gram faced every day. Her body could be healed but her mind couldn't."

"I'm sorry I didn't get to know Joridan." Sunev said, as they sat next to each other on the couch. "When I finally became myself again, so much time had passed, years in fact, I thought it best to leave you and your brother be. Mother, was right about one thing, those years with the Nerutas were the worst, the most savage.

It would *not* have been a good environment to raise two young children. I wasn't able to be a father at that time. And I don't expect to be one now, but I hope you'll allow me to be your friend."

"I'd like that," she'd answered.

He clasped her hands. "I really must get some sleep now. I'm an old man and need my rest."

Kiti laughed. If there was another man his age that looked as young as her father did, she'd never met him. He was about fifty-five but he only looked forty if that. At thirty-four, Peligro was eight years older than Kiti. Yet their father didn't look much older. If it hadn't been for Sunev's graying hair he could have been Peligro's brother rather than his father. Both of these new men in her life were tall and strong. Both reminded her of Joridan and her heart broke all over again as her determination to assess justice on Tybold grew.

The market teemed with activity on this the last day of the event. If they were going to get Tybold, it would have to be today.

The three of them went to the restaurant that had been agreed upon. They arrived early because Kiti was so nervous, she couldn't wait any longer. "What if he recognizes me? I've met him before. What if he--?"

"Kiti," said Sunev, "It doesn't matter. I have men posted around the plaza and in the restaurant. He will not escape me...er...us. Don't worry." He patted the hand she rested on the table.

"I'm trying. But he escaped once, he could do it again," she said matter-of-factly.

"It's true he did, but that's not happening this time," said Garrick. "Even if he does recognize us, it won't be as operatives from Centauri. It will be as kalcion traders, who've never left Procon. We tend to see what we want to see."

Kiti just nodded. Did she see what she wanted to see? Garrick caring. Garrick loving her. Was that real or just something she imagined because she wanted it so much?

"Kiti. Kiti!" Garrick's voice bought her back to reality. "Here they come."

Lord Tybold wore the most richly embroidered of his robes. Kiti recognized it as the robe he wore at Audra's wedding. Hopefully, she and Garrick, wouldn't be recognized but now was the test by fire, they'd been waiting for.

Sunev got up to greet them. "Lord Tybold and my beautiful Zia. How are you both this fine morning?" He slapped Tybold on the back, not too hard, the man would have been knocked over and gave Zia a kiss on the cheek. "Later," he whispered in her ear.

"Sunev, good to see you again. I understand this is your daughter and her husband." Tybold looked directly at Kiti.

"Yes they arrived yesterday from the Golong province. This is their first market and first sale from their mine." He leaned over conspiratorially and whispered in

Tybold's ear. "I gave it to them as a wedding present three years ago. It's taken them that long to get it built and producing."

Tybold looked down at Kiti. "Please to meet you Mrs…"

"Marcus, Kiti Marcus. I'm pleased to meet you Lord Tybold. Zia sings your praises."

Tybold took Kiti's proffered hand. Did he hold it a little too long? Look into her face a bit too close? Or was she imagining things?

Kiti removed her hand from his. "This is Garrick, my husband."

"Garrick Marcus. I know that name from somewhere."

Garrick offered his hand. "I can't imagine where. I've never been away from Procon. Kiti and I were both born and raised here."

"Of course," said Tybold, giving Garrick a limp handshake.

"Shall we get down to business? How much kalcion do you need?" Garrick asked.

"All you can sell me," answered Tybold.

"We have quite a lot to sell. This is our first year at the market and we have three years worth of kalcion to sell. Approximately one million tons. That will make a lot of swords. Enough for an army. Are you outfitting the Delazin army?" Garrick asked as nonchalantly.

"No. Why would you think we are from Delaz? We

are Centaurian and I am definitely not giving swords to their army either."

"My apologies. Zia said yesterday you came from Delaz."

"So we did. But originally we are from Centauri. I am in the Senate there. Lord Chancellor of the Senate as a matter of fact. We're going to outfit one of our ships with shields made from kalcion. I believe it will give us greater protection from the weapons of space pirates than we currently have."

"Really," said Garrick. "It sounds like a very interesting experiment. The government will guarantee your funds then?"

"Of course. I have the downpayment here." He patted the bag he carried on his shoulder.

"There. You see." Sunev said. "I told you he would be good for the funds."

"So you did and so did Zia." Kiti put her hand through the crook of the other woman's elbow. "Come let's sit down and order some food and wine. They have the most wonderful noskberry wine from Centauri. You've probably had it often, but it is new to Procon." She leaned in and whispered. "It is supposed to come from the Queen's own winery."

Kiti watched Garrick question her with his eyes. "Excuse me for a moment. My husband and I must confer."

"What?" asked Kiti.

"Where did you get another bottle of wine?"

"Audra actually gave me a case." Kiti admitted. "I'm using it to bait the trap."

"I hope you save a bottle for tonight. I'm going to need a reward"

"I have your reward, ready, willing and able." She reached up and stroked his chin. "Don't worry, it will be okay."

"I'm not worried. I'll cold cock the man if I need to but he's not leaving my sight again until he's safely in the brig on my ship. Though I would prefer it legally. I don't want there to be any chance he could get off on a technicality. "

"They appear to be arguing," said Tybold. "I was surprised to hear that you have a daughter and one fully grown as well. I never would've suspected."

"Yes, I haven't seen her for three years. Not since I gave them the deed to that mine on their wedding day. I have missed a great deal, not seeing her more often."

"Why didn't she come for a visit?" asked Tybold.

"It is an arduous one month journey to and from the mine. We don't have spaceships and transporters as you do. They did not want to take that much time away from their new enterprise."

"Quite true, Father. As much as I'd liked to have come home for a visit, taking two months out of each year would have set us back too far to be able to attend this market. Our production schedule wouldn't have been met and we would have had to wait another year. We couldn't afford to do that. Our beras have run out, so when Zia said you'd give us five percent above market, well you can imagine, we are ecstatic."

"Yes, I can imagine you were." Tybold turned and shot daggers at Zia. "That is what I get for letting Zia negotiate for me."

"You told me—" sputtered Zia.

"Enough," said Tybold. He started to backhand her but stopped as if remembering where he was. "We'll discuss this later."

Kiti looked up, "Ah, here come our friends." Peligro, Melana and Santro approached the table.

"Lord Tybold. May I present, my sister-in-law Melana, my brother Peligro and our friend Santro. I believe you've met Peligro before, is that not correct?

Kiti watched Tybold's manner go from sure of himself to panicked in little more than a second.

Peligro spoke. "Tybold of Centauri, you are under arrest for assault on my wife, Melana. You will rise and come with me peacefully."

Tybold reached for his comulator. "Transport me now. Now. I said transport me now."

"Your ship can no longer hear you I'm afraid," said Peligro. "I've taken over all control of the ship."

"Only until I can get my men on board," said Garrick.

"I thought I recognized you." Tybold said, then he whipped around and looked at Kiti. "Kitari Dolana. I know you, but you have his eyes. How is that possible? You are Centaurian."

"I wondered how long it would take for you to recognize me. I am Proconian. My parents are both from here. I was raised on Centauri by my grandmother. You, Lord Tybold, are going back to Centauri, after you are tried here for Melana's assault. You tried to pin it on Zia, knew that they would think it was she trying to get into Peligro's bed. What were you looking for? Hmm? Maps? Money?"

"What!! What are you talking about? I know nothing of any assault or attack on anyone. I have done nothing," yelled Zia. "Let me go. Take your hands off me."

"Nothing except kidnap the Queen of Centauri and give her to Slavarien to be tortured. No, you have done nothing at all. You will also return to Centauri to answer charges." Kiti spat. Her anger rising with each lying word that the woman uttered.

"Nooo. This can't be happening. Twice I should have been Queen. It's not fair. I've done so much, sacrificed, fucked every old, wrinkled man I had to for that to happen and now what. I go to jail for kidnapping. It's not fair."

"No you go to jail for conspiracy to commit murder."

"Murder? I never killed anybody. I just brought the Princess to Zelton. That's all. I didn't kill anyone."

"But Zelton did and you were his accomplice," said Kiti, trying to get her emotions back under control.

Garrick turned to Tybold. "Lord Tybold, I arrest you

on behalf of her Majesty Queen Dayanara for the murder of Joridan Dolana and twenty-eight other men and women."

"This can't be happening." Tybold sputtered. "Those stupid Slavarien brothers. If they'd done what they were supposed to do, you wouldn't be here or I'd be arresting you for treason. I know you would throw in with those Coridian's. Why couldn't Zelton have taken them out that he was supposed to? I'd never have given the intelligence report had I known that Anton Coridian would escape the trap."

"You bastard," Kiti screeched as she launched herself at Tybold. She gave him a right upper cut followed by a left jab and then jammed her right knee into his groin. He never knew what hit him before he fell to the ground writhing in pain.

"Kiti," Garrick grabbed her. "Kiti, my love, calm yourself."

Kiti was breathing hard. Her anger and grief having finally gotten the best of her. "He...I...I couldn't take it any longer. His snide looks and remarks. Speaking of what he did like it was of no more consequence than swatting a bug."

"I know." Garrick held her. "It's all right, love, it's all right."

Sunev's men took Tybold and Zia into custody.

"You haven't heard the last of me," yelled Tybold.

"Yes, we have." Garrick said quietly to Kiti. "I want you to go home on the Dremel."

"And you? You're not going home yet are you?" She shook her head. "Well I'm not either. I'll see them convicted of Melana's assault and then I will accompany you home on the Dremel or the Tangipahoa. I don't care which, but I'm not leaving without you."

"Yes, you are. You've been through enough."

"Yes, I have, so don't do this to me. I need closure. I need this, Garrick. You know I need this."

Garrick wrapped her in his arms. "All I want is for you to be safe. I want you to put this all behind you like it never happened. I want you to be happy."

"You want me to forget all that's happened?" Kiti heard what he said, but her brain registered, 'He doesn't love me. It was all for my father's benefit'.

"Yes. Forget it and move on."

Garrick knew he'd said something wrong. Kiti became wooden in his arms. She pushed away from him. "I think I will take the Dremel and go back home. I can fill in the royal family while you bring Tybold and Zia back after their trial here."

"Good." He said wondering what he'd done.

Kiti walked away.

Sunev walked up to Garrick. "They are safe in custody. Peligro is accompanying them to the holding area and will take them back to Zolthor for trial. It should be complete and we will have them back to you within the next two weeks. We have little crime, so our justice system is very swift."

Garrick nodded but never took his eyes off Kiti who left with Melana back to Sunev's home.

"Where is Kiti going?"

"Back to Centauri. I told her to forget what has happened and move on with her life, now that we have Tybold and Zia in custody."

"You told her to forget what has happened? You expect her to forget her brother's death. Or did you just want her to forget that you told me you would marry her?"

"What? No. I just meant to forget all the injustice. We have the perpetrators in custody and justice will now be served. She can be happy for that. We can be happy. I didn't mean. Oh, Krios!! I'm such an idiot."

"Yes, you are. My guess is that she is already on the Dremel and headed home. She had a comulator with her and I'm sure transported to the ship as soon as she was out of sight."

Garrick took off at a run for Sunev's house. He shoved through people but got delayed at the exit. The market was closing down and everyone was trying to leave at once. He had to push his way through. By the time he got to Sunev's house, Melana told him Kiti was gone.

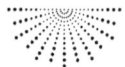

CHAPTER TEN

*S*unev was wrong. It took nearly a month for the trials to be over but Tybold and Zia were convicted on Procon for assault. They sat in his brig now. The Tangipahoa was making good time and would reach Centauri spaceport tonight. After he was sure that Darius had the prisoners safely in custody, he would go see Kiti. Explain that he didn't mean for her to forget Joridan or forget that he asked her to marry him. That he'd meant every word

Damn, his wayward mouth. Why didn't he think before he said things. He was sure if she just listened and gave him a chance that all would be well. She would understand what he meant. He'd tell her he loved her and didn't want to live without her. That he had asked her to marry him because he wanted to not because of any threat by Sunev.

Darius met the Tangipahoa with a full squad of

Dragonera to take the prisoners to jail where they would await trial for murder and treason. There was no way that either Tybold or Zia would be able to get out of this one.

"Have you seen Kiti? Is she with Audra?" Garrick asked Darius.

"No. She is gone, my friend."

"Gone? But where?"

"She is head of the diplomatic mission to Procon. When she got back a month ago, she told Audra about her father and brother, the new kalcion applications and requested permission to set up diplomatic and trade relations with Procon. Audra agreed immediately."

"When did she leave?"

"She's been gone for two weeks. You would have passed the Dremel in space."

"Damn. Darius, I need to go back to Procon. Can I have your permission to take the Tangipahoa?"

"I should say no. I don't know what you did, but Kiti cried for two days on Audra's shoulder. Do you know what that did to my sex life? It made it non-existent, because Audra became angry with me because you are my friend."

"I'm her friend too, dammit."

"Yes, she finally remembered that and remembered how rocky our courtship was. She demanded that I send you straight back to Procon as soon as you arrived. So get back on that ship and get going. She's got two weeks head start and by the time you get there, she's going to have had all that time to let her anger fester and build. You have a rough time ahead of you, my friend, if you want to get her back."

"Yes. But she's worth it. I may not have a lifemate like you and Anton, but Kiti is my heart and my soul. I can't live without her and I'm going to convince her of that, if it takes the rest of my life."

"Sounds to me like she is your lifemate, whether you realize it or not. That's the same way that Anton and I feel about our wives. We simply knew it a lot sooner than you, but the result is the same. Now go."

"Goodbye Darius. And thank you. The next time you see me, I'll be married to Kiti. I won't return until she agrees and the deed is done.

G arrick arrived back are Procon and went straight to Sunev's to see Kiti.

"Where is she?" He asked as he barged past Sunev.

"It took you long enough to get back here," his future father-in-law said to him. "I wasn't sure how long I would be able to stand it. She's made me teach her the way of the sword. She practices all day, every day, sparring with me, Peligro and Santro.

"Where is she?" Garrick repeated. He didn't care about her sword lessons or if she was wearing out her father with her sparring. All he cared about was getting to Kiti and talking to her.

"I'm getting to that," said Sunev. "Follow me."

"Fine." Garrick growled.

"Every night she barely eats. Since she's been back, she's lost weight and gained a lot of strength. She is a lot like her—"

"If you say she's a lot like you, I might have to belt you."

"She's a lot like her mother," Sunev finished. "Dolana was the most stubborn woman I've ever known, but she was the only one for me."

"Where. Is. Kiti?" Garrick was losing his patience.

"I'm getting to that." They walked back through the hidden living quarters in Sunev's home. "She hasn't been out of her room since I told her the Tangipahoa was in orbit. She's in there stewing, my boy, and she's armed. Can you use a sword?"

"I don't need a sword. Kiti won't hurt me."

"Son, she wants to kill you. Sure you don't want my sword?"

"I'm sure. But there is something you can do."

"What? Anything, if it will get my girl back to her normal sweet self."

"Have your theologian ready to marry us when we come out."

"Certainly are sure of yourself, aren't you?"

"Kiti loves me, she may not know it yet, but she will before we come out of there and she will be sure that I love her. Oh and don't be alarmed if you hear things crashing. She may throw things but I assure you she won't use her sword on me."

Sunev laughed. "Perhaps you know her better than I thought."

"Yes, but she doesn't know me."

Sunev got serious and pinned Garrick to the wall. "You hurt her again, you will answer to me."

"Understood," said Garrick, shaking off Sunev's grasp.

"We're here." Sunev clapped Garrick on the back. "Good luck, Son. She is one pissed off woman."

"Thank you. I'm going to need it; I just don't know how much of it I'll need."

Garrick knocked on Kiti's door.

"Go away."

"No. Kiti let me in. We need to talk."

"About what? Are you going to tell me again that I need to forget what happened?"

"Yes."

The door flew open. Kiti stood there, the poster child for righteous indignation. "You want me to forget that Tybold murdered Joridan? Or that Zia kidnapped Audra right under my nose? Or that Slavarien tortured Anton?"

"No. That's not what I meant and you know it."

"Oh, you just want me to forget the part where you said you'd marry me. Well, consider it forgotten."

"Good. I never should have told Sunev I would marry you."

Kiti was crestfallen. Her face lost all its color. "Fine. I have forgotten. You can go back to your life as it was before."

"Good. I'm glad you understand. I wouldn't want there to be any misunderstandings between us."

"Of course. It would be awkward when we run into each other."

"Yes, it would."

"Fine. I won't be returning to Centauri for some time anyway."

"No, you won't."

"Fine. Goodbye."

"Kiti."

"What?" she snapped.

"Would you marry me?" He stepped in, closed the door and dropped to one knee. "Please be my wife."

Kiti shook her head. "You don't have to do this. I've spoken to Sunev. Explained that it was just the pressure of the moment."

Garrick rose. "Kiti," he took her in his arms. "Shut up."

There were unshed tears clinging to her eyelashes. Garrick kissed them away.

"Kitari Dolana, there is only one reason I want to marry you." He took her precious face in his hands. "I love you. I've loved you nearly all my life and I'm never going to let you go again."

She sniffled. "You love me? Really?"

"Yes. I love you. For forever and a day. You're my heart, my soul, my life. Without you there is only dark. Please don't send me to live in the dark. You are my light, Kiti. Marry me."

"Oh Garrick, I do love you. Yes. Yes, I'll marry you."

"Good. I don't think I could have restrained myself from kissing you much longer." He took her in his arms and kissed her, long and thoroughly. Then he picked her up in his arms and carried her to the bedroom.

He set her on her feet and she unfastened her vest before he moved her hands and stripped it down her arms. Her breasts lay exposed and unhindered for his plundering.

And plunder he did taking first one and then the other into his mouth. While he worked on at the fastening for her skirt with his hands.

Finally, he had her naked. His hands couldn't seem to get enough of her, moving up and over her stomach to her breasts and back again until she ached to feel him, all of him against her, skin to skin, heart to heart.

Kiti was so ready for him she thought she'd explode when he kissed her. Her hands clawed at his shirt, searching for the fasteners before he took pity on her and pulled it over his head.

Dark golden hair curled over his chest then down his stomach coming to a vee as it went under his waistband.

She followed it all the way down under the band with her hand until he stopped her

"I have you now," she said. The tip of his beautiful cock peaked out from the vee where the fastener ended. Unable to resist, she tongued it with the very hard pointed tip of her tongue.

He lifted her head till she looked at him. "Play fair."

"Not until you are naked, my love."

He shed his pants with lightening speed. "Come with me, Kiti." He took her hand and laid on the bed, pulling her down on top of him.

She positioned herself over him. "Come into me Garrick. I want you now, to feel you now."

Kiti slowly lowered herself onto his penis. Garrick lifted and thrust into her at the same time and Kiti felt herself tighten, ready to explode. "Fast Garrick, I need you fast and hard, I'm so ready and so close. Don't make me wait."

He complied with her urgent plea and slammed up into her, pumping in and out. Harder. Faster. Kiti arched her back and screamed.

Garrick followed her and Kiti felt his release deep within her womb.

She collapsed on top of him. "We have got to learn to take more time, but I can't seem to get you fast enough. I need you so much, I ache. Not just in my heart, but in my womb. I need you and only you can give me what I need. I love you, Garrick Marcus."

"We'll learn. We finally found each other and have all the time in the world."

Kiti cuddled in next to his big body, curving herself to fit against him. "I know, but we've wasted so much time on others, that we could have been together."

"No, Kiti. We spent time learning. Learning what our hearts really want, allowing us to find each other. It simply took us longer. Now we know what we want and who we are. There is nothing to come between us now."

"I guess you're right. I don't ever want to be with anyone else. I can't imagine it. But there are things I can imagine." She rolled away from him and kneeled on the bed. "Garrick."

"Hmm," said the well satisfied man.

"I want to do something different. I want you to enter me from behind. I want you to hit that spot that Audra told me about. It's called the G spot and the climax is supposed to be incredible"

Garrick laughed. "I want to love you in any and all ways. If you want me to hang upside down from the ceiling, that's what I'll do."

It was Kiti's turn to laugh. "I doubt that you passing out when all the blood rushes to your head would do anything for me."

Kiti got on all fours, Garrick on his knees behind her. He found the opening to her vagina and entered her slowly. This time they would go slow. She was determined. She'd been sated once already and wasn't in such a frenzy this time.

Garrick leaned over her, while entering and withdrawing, slow and deliberate, to the hilt each time. She felt him at the entrance to her womb with each thrust. He took her breasts in his hands, squeezing them gently and rolling the nipples between his thumb and forefinger.

Kiti felt herself tighten with each of Garrick's thrusts. He was definitely hitting a great spot. She didn't know if it was the G spot but it was a wonderful one. So close she could hardly stand it, she reached between her legs and rubbed her clitoris. It finished her off. She bucked, and then clamped so tight around Garrick, she was sure she'd hurt him till she heard him yell and felt his hot seed fill her.

They collapsed in a heap.

*ater, Garrick said, "We may have made a baby tonight. I didn't use any protection. Would that upset you? To have a baby right away?"

Kitty sighed. "Do you think so?" She patted her flat tummy. "No. It wouldn't upset me. I think it would be wonderful. I even have names picked out if you agree."

"What are the names?"

"Joridan for a boy and Dolana for a girl. What do you think?"

"I like them. Joridan Marcus and Dolana Marcus. Nice ring to them but not as good as Kitari Marcus.

Your father has his theologian waiting outside to marry us. I'm not taking a chance on losing you again. I've waited too long for you, Kiti. I can't wait any longer."

"Good. I love you Garrick."

"I love you, Kitari, for forever and a day."

STAY CONNECTED!

Newsletter

Sign up for my <u>newsletter</u> and get a free book.

Follow Cindy

https://www.facebook.com/cindy.woolf.5
https://twitter.com/CynthiaWoolf
http://cynthiawoolf.com

ABOUT THE AUTHOR

Cynthia Woolf is an award-winning and best-selling author of forty-five historical western romance novels and six sci-fi romance novels, which she calls westerns in space. Along with these books she has also published four boxed sets of her books.

Cynthia loves writing and reading romance. Her first western romance Tame A Wild Heart was inspired by the story her mother told her of meeting Cynthia's father on a ranch in Creede, Colorado. Although Tame A Wild Heart takes place in Creede that is the only similarity between the stories. Her father was a cowboy not a bounty hunter and her mother was a nursemaid (called a nanny now) not the owner of the ranch.

Cynthia credits her wonderfully supportive husband Jim and her great critique partners for saving her sanity and allowing her to explore her creativity.

ALSO BY CYNTHIA WOOLF

Bachelors and Babies

Carter

Cupids & Cowboys

Lanie

The Marshal's Mail Order Brides

The Carson City Bride

The Virginia City Bride

The Silver City Bride

Brides of Homestead Canyon/Montana Sky Series

Thorpe's Mail-Order Bride

Kissed by a Stranger

A Family for Christmas

Bride of Nevada

Genevieve

Brides of the Oregon Trail

Hannah

Lydia

Bella

Eliza

Rebecca

Charlotte

Brides of San Francisco

Nellie

Annie

Cora

Sophia

Amelia

Brides of Seattle

Mail Order Mystery

Mail Order Mayhem

Mail Order Mix-Up

Mail Order Moonlight

Mail Order Melody

Brides of Tombstone

Mail Order Outlaw

Mail Order Doctor

Mail Order Baron

Central City Brides

The Dancing Bride

The Sapphire Bride

The Irish Bride

The Pretender Bride

Destiny in Deadwood

Jake

Liam

Zach

Hope's Crossing

The Stolen Bride

The Hunter Bride

The Replacement Bride

The Unexpected Bride

Matchmaker & Co Series

Capital Bride

Heiress Bride

Fiery Bride

Colorado Bride

The Surprise Brides

Gideon

Tame

Tame a Wild Heart

Tame a Wild Wind

Tame a Wild Bride

Tame A Honeymoon Heart

Tame Boxset

Centauri Series (SciFi Romance)

Centauri Dawn

Centauri Twilight

Centauri Midnight

Singles

Sweetwater Springs Christmas

www.ingramcontent.com/pod-product-compliance
Lightning Source LLC
Chambersburg PA
CBHW070455130626
46555CB00003B/1017